BOMBAY TO MUMBAI

THE CRIME GAME

DINESH LIMBACHIYA

INDIA • SINGAPORE • MALAYSIA

Notion Press Media Pvt Ltd

No. 50, Chettiyar Agaram Main Road,
Vanagaram, Chennai, Tamil Nadu – 600 095

First Published by Notion Press 2022
Copyright © Dinesh Limbachiya 2022
All Rights Reserved.

ISBN 979-8-88530-375-0

Dedication

This Book is Dedicated to My Beloved Daughter
Ms SWETA.
We all Miss YOU Forever.
Your Loving Papa Dinesh, Mom Rita,
Harsh And Bharati.

PREFACE

A desire to write a book about my experiences was always on my mind.

I have often seen, heard and experienced crimes being committed, with Mumbai as its backdrop. This was the seventies and during this decade, newspapers were the only medium which connected people to the world of crime.

After spending the first six years of my life in the village, my father brought us back to Mumbai in the seventies. Our financial status was not very good so we shifted to Mumbai in the hope of making money. On our arrival, we immediately settled down in a single room in Bandukwala Chawl in Vikhroli Village. The room where we started our new life was very simple and small. But as a kid I was very happy in that small room too.

This area was well known for all sorts of illegal businesses. As young kids we noticed people smuggling local liquor inside tyre tubes. Quite often the police would come knocking at our landlord's door at night, to search his house, as he too was regularly involved in the smuggling. Even with this sort of atmosphere we were quite comfortable and happy.

After staying in Vikhroli for three years my father shifted us to Vidya Vihar, a suburb of Mumbai. Here too we were staying in a tenement but our monetary situation was much better. A suburb called Chembur was very close to our area and an area called Tilak Nagar was just next door. Bada Rajan reigned over this area. Rajan Bhai always held a lavish Puja for Lord Ganesha. People from far off places would come here, to pay their respect to the lord.

Sahakar Talkies (a popular movie theatre) was also nearby. This theatre exists even today and Rajan Bhai ruled this place too. To retain their hold on the theatre two different gangs often had a fight and many a times a few gang members would be killed too. By that time, I had grown up and was fourteen years of age.

The boys from Chembur used to come and sell film tickets in black at the Odeon Theatre in Ghatkopar area. This angered the local Maharashtrian boys and they would rush there, ready for a battle. Soda bottles and swords were often used in abundance in fights. There would be bloodshed too and as usually shown in films, the police would come towards the end of the battle. Only to find broken soda bottles and blood on the street. The cops would inquire but nobody would give any answers. Everybody was scared of these boys.

The main reason for this arson was the large amount of money they would earn by selling the tickets in black.

During that era it was unfortunate that most of the crimes were committed in Odeon theatre, which was a place of entertainment. For some time the theatre license was also cancelled.

As time passed the situation in my family slowly improved. It was not that tense anymore. Our financial situation was also improving with time. Now people got to watch crime reports on television. During those days another business was doing very well, the Kalyanji matka (matka is a form of betting and lottery). This business too was successfully running at every nook and corner. Now this city was slowly changing. Its journey from Bombay to Mumbai had started. New styles of crime were being invented. This was a time when crime was escalating and getting more and more murkier.

The younger generation was getting attracted to this life of crime. They would join a gang of their choice and get involved in all types of criminal activities including murders. They were ready to kill with just an indication from their bosses. They were their puppets in this game of bloodshed. During those days, one would often hear a name, Rajan Nair aka Bad Rajan. Chota Rajan used to sell movie tickets in black at the time and he earned a good amount of money.

Television and newspapers were full of biased statements made by a big politician. He would openly state that he was partial towards one community. His statements often created a stir in the world of journalism. His dislike for the UPites (a person from Uttar Pradesh, India) was a well-known fact. In 1980 the UPites built thousands of huts in kalina near the Air India Colony and they started dealing in scrap materials,black oil.

The politicians were not happy about this. Though the Government made them vacate the area, the Meethi River was already contaminated by then.

When Bade Rajan was killed in 1983, I was twenty one years old. The whole area was shocked by this killing. Many rumours were spreading like now his men will avenge his death. It would be an eye for an eye. Now Chota Rajan would take over Bada Rajan's business. There would be dozens of killings. After this killing, as time passed, more of these mishaps occured. My mind was full of these incidents. I always collected all newspaper clippings during this time.

My father and his love for books inspired me to write. When I sat down to write this book, two things helped me, my father's words of wisdom to me and the clippings I had saved. When I started writing this book I remembered so many people who had passed away. I continued to write with the aid of my memories and I aligned them with the contemporary times also.

But one of the main reasons to write this book was a hope in my heart, that this journey of crime would come to an end.

BOMBAY TO MUMBAI – The Crime Game

Bombay has always been a city of dreams. People from all walks of life and all over India have been coming to Bombay to fulfill their dreams and better their lives.

Bombay is a city for which many people have sung praises of appreciation and will continue to do so for generations to come. This land is so fertile that no matter what you sow you are bound to get great results.

Many Gujaratis arrived in Bombay from Gujarat in the 1850s. With no road transport, it was not an easy journey to make. People from Porbandar and Kutch would travel by boats via the oceanic route and many trudged for miles to reach Bombay.

All they carried with them was a lota (a brass pot), a thick rope and some dry snacks for the road, enough to last them through the long trip. If they came across a well during their journey, they would draw water with the help of the rope and the lota and quench their hunger and thirst.

After this difficult journey, the adventurous and fearless Gujarati would finally make his way to Mumbai and start toiling tirelessly to set up their business.

This authenticity and integrity was their hallmark and they prospered immensely because of it. Their prosperity helped Mumbai prosper too. They had come to Mumbai with just a rope and a lota and changed history. There is a saying in Gujarati 'I had come to Mumbai with just a dhoti to wear and a lota in hand, and look how I have prospered'. To this day, Gujaratis say this about their forefathers who came to Mumbai. Today the streets of Mumbai have been named after them and also huge buildings and hospitals have been built by them. All of this helped Mumbai attain the grandeur it is known for today.

As Mumbai reached its peak of grandeur, swindlers were around to steal it too. Conmen activity gained momentum and the foundation of "Chor Bazaar" was laid. This goes on even today and they are unstoppable. Many lost their lives struggling for their place under the sun.

Criminals only followed one simple law, the 'jungle law', where MIGHT WAS RIGHT and this is how it works even today. But then there was a change. The cowardly criminals with their cunning brains, who were as sharp as a vile fox, started ruling over the ignorant criminals who gave up their peace, tranquility and their lives too like slaves. The so-called "Dons" would hide like rats in their holes or in Dubai and kept their hold over Mumbai for decades.

But a few fearless criminals did not hide, did not flee and nor did they betray their country. Although this was in the good old days. Each of them had their own era, their own rules. While a few remained immortal in people's hearts, others lost their place on the earth.

Many Dons have arrived on the land of crime and terrorism in Mumbai and then vanished in thin air. But a few are still in the news and one of them is Purshottam Panara. His great grandfather arrived in Mumbai from Navsari, a small town in Gujarat. His father was a judge and therefore Purshottam chose law as his career, but he was always attracted to the world of crime, right from his student days. One of the reasons for this attraction could be because their dinner time conversations always centered around criminals and their history.

Today he is known as the infamous Purshottam Panara aka Vakil Saab in the criminal world. His visiting card reads Purshottam Panara, Governor of Supreme Court, India and he has an office in Malad but his actual work starts at Sonali Bar at 10 in the night. Vakil Saab is 5 feet 10 inch and he weighs nearly 125 kilos. His body is a little on the heavier side, like any 45 year old.

A table is always reserved for Vakil Saab at the bar. The moment he enters the bar, the dance and the orchestra always stops as a sign of respect. Today too the dancing stopped. Vakil Saab took his seat and announced "let the dance begin." The artists were waiting for this sign and the entertainment began. Vakil Saab was a dare devil but he was a romantic too. He was in love with a singer from Mirzapur. Her name was Reshma Billi. She had a place in his heart and shared his bed too.

She was beautiful and sang like a nightingale. It was her childhood dream to become a playback singer and she knew that Vakil Saab was the easiest way to the filmy world she had always dreamt of.

As usual, Vakil Saab gave Adil a few bundles of cash and he started showering them on the dancers as a sign of appreciation. People from different walks of life were there to seek Vakil Saab's advice. On one hand he would be solving their disputes while on the other, he would be happily sipping his drink. Many people who were exploited and swindled came to him asking for his help and he helped them too. However there was one case in particular that was troubling him and he was losing his sleep over it. Bhau, a well known don's son Rupesh had usurped a Sindhi builder Prakash Nainani's land. Vakil Saab tried to settle the dispute and called Rupesh for meetings but he was adamant about it. He was demanding 20 crores to vacate the land. But the builder Prakash Nainani could only afford to pay him 1.5 crores.

Vakil Saab was constantly thinking about this case. He could have solved the problem in a twisted way but he was a man of principles so it was difficult for him to do anything drastic.

That same day a weird looking, thin man approached him and said "I want to talk to Vakil Saab." Aadil, who was standing near Vakil Saab asked "What do you want to talk about?." The weird man said "I will talk only with Vakil Saab." Vakil Saab took another sip from his glass and said "sit down, tell me about your problem." But he just stood there, full of arrogance and said "I never have a problem. I solve other's problems." Gurudas, Vakil Saab's right hand man heard this and roared "are you drunk? You are talking utter nonsense." The weird man did not even glance at Gurudas and continued talking to Vakil Saab. "Saab my name is Rampal. You give me just one chance, I'll move heaven and earth for you and make them meet. I can make impossible things possible for you."

Aadil heard this and thought to himself that this man must be a druggie. He does not know what he is talking about. Aadil did not want such riff raffs wasting Vakil Saab's precious time, he said "If you have come to have some fun then this will be your last time....."

Vakil Saab interrupted him and immediately said "What can you do for me"

Rampal replied "Anything"

Vakil Saab told him about the issue with the builder's plot.

Rampal immediately said "It will be done. Who is occupying the plot?"

Gurudas told him that Rupesh Kumar had usurped it. He also told him that he was demanding 25 crores for it.

Rampal asked" How much are you ready to pay?"

"Only 1.5 crore. My builder cannot afford more than that…" said Vakil Saab. Rampal asked him "Where is the plot?" Gurudas jumped in and said, "It's on the Jogeshwari-Vikhroli Link road." "Ok, done", said Rampal. "You reach the place at 10 tomorrow morning and I promise your work will be done." The moment Aadil heard this he said "If you are not there tomorrow, I will scour heaven and earth till I find you and will shoot you point blank." On hearing this Rampal shot back at him, "Tell the builder to be ready to do the Pooja tomorrow" and without waiting for an answer, he turned and left.

Aadil was staring at his receding back and was thinking whether he will actually come tomorrow. Vakil Saab's sixth sense read Aadil's mind and said "He will definitely come tomorrow." Vakil Saab was good at prophesying about future events and he felt sure about Rampal.

The next day Vakil Saab reached the appointed place in his car. Gurudas and Aadil were also with him. Builder Prakash Nainani was right behind them in his grand Mercedez. Purshottam had only one thought in his mind, will Rampal come?

A few more minutes passed and the thought turned into a niggling doubt. He could sense builder Nainani's impatience as he was constantly looking at his 'status symbol', his costly and imported watch.

As Aadil saw Nainani getting antsy he alighted from his car. He himself was beginning to get a little restless. Gurudas' thoughts were also disturbed. Prakash Nainani's gaze was shifting from his watch to Aadil, who was pacing impatiently. Gurudas and Vakil Saab were sitting in the car waiting for something to happen.

Suddenly out of nowhere, a jeep barged into the compound with a trail of wind and dust. It had broken the gate and crashed on its way in.

Rupesh heard the loud sound and came running out with his revolver and 10 to 15 of his cronies followed him. The dust was still up in the air as Rampal alighted from the jeep, unarmed. He said "I am Rampal. You must have received Bhau's call by now. Come on, all of you get out. Just leave. Vacate the place. Now." The moment they heard Rampal's name the cronies were so scared that they ran away immediately. They knew exactly how sour Bhau and Rampal's relations were. Rupesh glared at Rampal with rage, then looked at Aadil and left the place immediately.

But before he left he looked back with an undeniable fruitless arrogant attitude and said "you just don't know what you have done. You have snatched a prey from my mouth." Aadil simply smiled. If only looks could kill, Rupesh would have been dead by now. Aadil's smile poured a thin stream of acid down Rupesh's throat as he was leaving. Vakil Saab was baffled at the turn of events and how easily the plot was vacated. Rampal came up to him and told him that he had done his job as he had promised. "Where is my payment?" he quipped. Vakil Saab turned his eyes towards the builder Prakash Nainani. Nainani simply smiled and like a true Sindhi, said "Here it is Sai. The full 1.5 crore, you can count it Sai." Rampal took the bag of money and said, "I can't disrespect Vakil Saab, I trust him implicitly. I don't want to count the amount." Saying this he put the bag in his broken rickety jeep and vanished into thin air.

Vakil Saab was looking at the dust storm left behind by the jeep. He still could not fathom how Rampal managed to get Rupesh to vacate the plot so easily. He wondered who this Rampal was.

Vakil Saab pushed these thoughts away as Prakash Nainani opened the champagne bottle which he had brought with him and poured a little on the ground. Today his happiness knew no bounds. Vakil Saab and Nainani had just started celebrating their success with sips of champagne when suddenly Aadil's mobile phone rang. He answered the call and his face suddenly fell. Vakil Saab saw this and asked him "why do you look upset?" Aadil could not utter a single word. He gathered some strength and mumbled "Judge Saab has left us to meet his creator." The glass of champagne fell from Vakil Saab's hand and his mind went blank. He was shocked.

The news of Judge Saab's death spread like wildfire. The moment people heard the news, they shut their shops and businesses and joined his funeral.

Judge Saab was held in great respect by people who knew him well. It is never very easy to reach that height of popularity and do so much charity. He had done a lot of charity work in his lifetime. He had helped guide many people in their careers and helped them during their bad times, by showing them different paths of life to success. While there were a few amongst them who did not agree with Vakil Saab's ideology, they were impressed with Judge Saab's personality and reputation. Both father and son lived different styles of life but they had only one goal in mind - social service, fighting against injustice and helping people fight for their rights. Judge Saab never stopped Vakil Saab from operating his business the way he did. He knew that whichever way Vakil Saab went his sole goal in life was social service. Hoards of people attended Judge Saab's funeral. His personality was like a huge sequoia tree with its branches spread around, protecting the poor and needy who needed his support.

He was like a Godfather protecting people who worked for him. He was never interested in any monetary gains. People who loved him unfailingly closed their commercial shops showing their respect and loyalty towards him.

After the formal rituals were over Vakil Saab went to Kashi to immerse his ashes according to the religious diktat. A few people from the district of 'Dang', including their village Sarpanch and a few other big names accompanied him to complete this final rite.

After 12 days of mourning period Vakil Saab went to his ancestral home in the village with his Mother. Vakil Saab gazed at the old walls with a lot of love. When he saw the broken fountain in the compound he was reminded of his childhood days. Their old ambassador car was still sitting in the courtyard as a reminder of the past glory. Judge Saab went to the court every day in this very car from the same courtyard. When he was nominated as the Supreme Court Judge the same courtyard had witnessed a gala event, a lavish party. The gentlemen and the criminals, both shared the same table and food too. Judge Saab loved greenery around him so he had employed a gardener and he would plant a lot of trees which had now outgrown and spread over the walls. Today it looked as if they were stretching their branches out, giving shade to the neglected and deserted mansion. He was not the only one who was orphaned but there were many who were left without a strong support. of Judge Saab. As he entered the house all the memories came rushing back.

As the mother and son entered Purshottam noticed Judge Saab's almirah. The moment he opened the almirah he saw Judge Saab's licensed revolver lying there.

Vakil Saab owned a lot of illegal(benami) weapons, but he did not know about his father owning one. His mother saw his shock and told him very calmly, "When you were hardly ten years old, Judge Saab had punished a criminal by imposing a life sentence on him. The criminal lost his temper and threatened Judge Saab in a loud voice saying, "Arre oye judge, you better take care of your son." This made Judge Saab ask the Government for a licensed revolver to protect you." Vakil Saab's gaze was transfixed on the revolver imagining the situation and his father's anguish. His eyes were misty as his gaze shifted to the other almirah.

He opened it gingerly and he saw a collection of old alcohol bottles. Most of them were bottles of undistilled liquor which were at least 25 years old. These bottles were sealed by molten lac in those old days. The bottle had labels written in Gujarati. It read "Jeeva kala Desi kaju Daru, Bhikha Patel desi Jambu Daru, Madha Khepa Santara Deshi Daru. All the alcohol was manufactured in different districts of Navsari, Valsad and Vapi. Maheru Daru came from the Banaskantha district with a label stating Mehru Daru and the manufacturer's name was Keshav Rathod. This desi alcohol did not taste any less than the foreign scotch whiskey. During British rule many Britishers specially ordered this alcohol. The Britishers who showed off and loved their scotch would order the desi alcohol for their personal consumption on the sly and it was also imported in those days. Maa and Vakil Saab kept gazing at the beautiful bottles of the local alcohol. Judge Saab loved to have this local alcohol and he had it all his life. Maa said "Now that judge Saab is no more, what will we do with these bottles?" Just then a bottle rolled out of the almirah and almost dropped but Vakil Saab immediately bent down and grabbed the bottle before it could touch the floor. He took the bottle in his hand and caressed it and said "Maa, I have inherited it. I am the only heir of these priceless bottles. This is a gift from my father. He always gave away things to people, so I love this gift."

Judge Saab had always done charity for the tribals of a district called 'Dang'. He had donated a huge amount of money so that the poor children from that district could get proper education and constructed dispensaries so that people would not die due to minor illnesses. Many felt orphaned after Judge Saab's death. Vakil Saab too missed him a lot.

Anyway Vakil Saab was not the type to mourn for long, so today, 15 days after his father's death, Vakil Saab had come to the office to start his normal routine. Builder Prakash Nainani's construction work was in full swing and the Vakil gang was very excited. The Vakil gang had three flats booked in their name already.

As Vakil Saab entered his office, the first thing he did was put a garland on his father's photo frame. As he was putting the garland he casually looked out of the nearby window and saw a Sadhu walking down the road. Vakil Saab immediately recognised him. The same Sadhu had predicted about two years back that Vakil Saab would lose one of his parents. Vakil Saab quickly ordered Aadil to call the Sadhu in his office. The moment the Sadhu Mahatma entered his office he recognized Vakil Saab and said "One year ago you had given me food, I still have to pay back that obligation. Do you want something from me? Vakil Saab told him "I lost my father 15 days back." The Sadhu simply smiled and said "People come and go. That is a normal routine of this world. If you want to ask something you can do so without any hesitation." To which Vakil Saab replied "Mahatmaji, I just need your blessings. I have all the worldly luxuries I need. You tell me what I can do for you?" After a good thought Mahatmaji said "I want to go to the Kailas Mansarovar for a pilgrimage which will cost more than a lac." After saying these words, Mahatmaji sat there silently. Vakil Saab too, silently opened his almirah and then walked over to the Sadhu Mahatma and put a bundle of two lacs in a cotton sling bag which he was carrying. "You have made this Sadhu very happy" said Mahatmaji and he added "You love sadhus. You have an affinity towards sadhus. You have the courage to walk on razor sharp edges where cowards don't dare to walk. Today you are attracted towards crime but a day will come when you will be tired of it. You are not just a normal human being. You are a mixture of so many personalities. You are a devil but you are also a saint. You are enjoying the fruits of your father's charity, his good deeds. People will remember you for generations. As he was saying these words he noticed Aadil and Gurudas standing nearby. He kept staring at them for a little while and said "These two will change the direction of your life. Shiv, the soul and Shiva, the destroyer in your life shall meet when this pair will split.

After saying this the Mahatma got up abruptly and said "Do you have any more questions? This is going to be our last meeting." Vakil Saab simply joined hands in respect and said "No Mahatmaji" Mahatmaji rose from his chair and said "Ok then, I will take your leave now. I still have to return your obligation."

As soon as the Sadhu Mahatma left Aadil noticed a Rudraksha mala lying on the table and he exclaimed "Mahatmaji has forgotten his mala!" Vakil Saab immediately sent Aadil and Gurudas in different directions but they could not find him anywhere. As they returned to his office Aadil said "Maybe the Mahatma left the mala for you" Gurudas agreed with him and added "Yes Vakil Saab, maybe Mahatmaji left this mala as a 'prasad' (sacrement) for you. He did mention that this is a final meeting."

Vakil Saab touched the mala to his forehead as a token of respect and wrapped it around his wrist.

That same day Vakil Saab arrived at Sonali's Bar. It had been 15 days since he had been there and it was time for celebration at the bar. Many people flocked around him, welcomed him and came to pay their respects. Vakil Saab was very happy today as he had done his pious duty, by sending the Mahatma to Kailash for a tour. The girls at the bar were dancing as usual and Vakil Saab had given Aadil and Gurudas two bundles of cash as usual when suddenly out of nowhere, Rampal appeared and put a bag full of cash on the table which was unusual. As he put the bag down he said "this is your share, 25 lacs for you." Vakil Saab looked up and asked Rampal, "My share?" Rampal replied "Yes Vakil Saab, I have been very impressed with your principles. You may not know me but I have always considered you as my 'guru'. This bag full of cash is my 'guru dakshina', a way of paying my respect for whatever I have learnt from you without your knowledge. I don't belong to any gang. This is your share of the cash the builder paid me."

This sentence reminded Vakil Saab of the Mahatma, and the entire scene flashed before his eyes again. He realised that the Mahatma had put him through a test by asking for cash for his pilgrimage. Saints like him are not at all interested in money. He looked up at Aadil and he told him "Mahatmas like him never keep any debt pending." Vakil Saab closed his eyes and touched the mala to his forehead and took a deep breath. He suddenly felt immense peace and a type of tranquility he had never experienced before. He felt as if he was enveloped in the aura of the Mahatma's presence.

After Vakil Saab met Rampal that day he realised that Rampal was very faithful. In just a few meetings his sincerity impressed Vakil Saab. Rampal had created an important place in Vakil Saab's heart. At the same time Rampal too was impressed by Vakil Saab and wanted to work for him forever. He gained Vakil Saab's trust within a few months and soon the two became a famous duo.

Since the time they started working closely, Rampal and Vakil Saab's names were often mentioned amongst the underworld criminals in whispers. Their names became famous beyond the borders too and created a sense of fear amongst the terrorists. The news of their partnership was spread fast by traitors who were friends with criminals across the borders.

With news like these floating around Vakil Saab had created more foes than friends. The Lawyers Union tried to ban Vakil Saab from practising law, as his name was associated with crime. At the time Vakil Saab stated with a lot of confidence that the day they show the proof of his involvement in any crime, he will not only quit his profession, but he will leave Mumbai too. It was unfortunate that Rampal worked for a swindler like Bhau earlier and that is why he was sentenced for life about which we will talk later.

Rampal however, ended up being sentenced for life and he was out on parole. But after he joined Vakil Saab he reopened his case and managed to change his life sentence to just a few years of imprisonment. As Rampal had already spent a few years in the prison he was allowed to go free

The next day Vakil Saab's name had made it to the headlines of the topmost newspapers. His name had been added to the list of the lawyers who helped criminals. After what he did with Rampal's case, other criminals who were sentenced for life had high hopes of getting a reprieve. All of them wanted Vakil Saab as their lawyer.

Now Rampal would be in prison for only three more years. He always prayed for Vakil Saab's well being and wanted to work as his servant forever. He decided to dedicate his whole life to looking after Vakil Saab.

After a busy day Vakil Saab would often go to Madh Island with Reshma Billi to relax and indulge in some romance. Both would drive down the quiet road. The salty breeze coming from the sea and being surrounded by the lush green forest around felt very peaceful. It seemed as if one had left the hustle bustle of the city far behind.

Today, he was returning from one such trip with Reshma Billi. It was almost daybreak. The roads of Madh Island were slowly waking up. Dewdrops were shining through the faint sunlight on the leaves and were slowly trickling down. The dry leaves were rustling in the breeze. Vakil Saab was enjoying both the wine and the woman and the beautiful atmosphere engulfed him making him even more happy and relaxed.. Reshma was sleeping with her head resting on Vakil Saab's chest. Vakil Saab was driving the car at a very slow pace. With the windows down the soft cool breeze was creating an intoxicating atmosphere. In this beautiful silence you could only hear their two hearts beating as one. Suddenly a bullet pierced this silence and whizzed past, shattering the wind screen and missing Vakil Saab's temple. Vakil Saab missed death by an inch. He could not grasp what was happening. He increased the speed of his car. In a split second another bullet hit the car, shattering the rear windshield. Now Reshma was really scared. She clung on to Vakil Saab as if her life depended on him. Vakil Saab wrapped his arms around Reshma and kept her close to him and increased the speed of his car as he sensed that Reshma was scared to death.

Vakil Saab's name was once again in the headlines the next day. Aadil was sifting through all the informants as quickly as he could to get to the person who had dared to attack Vakil Saab. It looked as if the shooter had vanished into thin air. Aadil tried his level best to find the culprit but he did not succeed and the whole affair died down after a few days. However, Aadil decided to keep this incident always etched in his memory.

Aadil and Gurudas both were Vakil Saab's strength. Many criminals were trying to break up this pair which would make Vakil Saab very vulnerable. All the gangs were waiting for that to happen so that they could overcome Vakil Saab. In this world full of criminals everybody wanted to earn some green bucks and they thought that they would earn a little more by breaking Vakil Saab down. Many gangs tried to break their camaraderie but they failed miserably. Aadil and Gurudas, both held Vakil Saab in high esteem and he too took care of them like a father. The Vakil gang was not just a gang but a family too. Gurudas was a staunch Ganesh devotee so he would visit Siddhivinayak temple regularly and Aadil would visit the Paidro Baba's dargah near Victoria Terminus station every Thursday and pay his respects. Aadil always felt peace and tranquility when he visited the dargah. It was believed that a Britisher had built this dargah. Aadil would also do his share of charity amongst the poor people here This gang was not afraid of the police. They were out in the open, doing their nefarious activities without a care with full faith in their various Gods.

Today Vakil Saab did not go to Sonali bar, his regular haunt. He stayed at home enjoying the country liquor he had inherited from his father. His mother saw him sitting with a bottle in hand and she said "Purshottam, please give me some cash. I want to donate it to the temple. "Vakil Saab said "take it from my pocket. "When she opened the pocket she saw there were two bundles of notes lying in his pocket.

She asked Purshottam "Aren't you going to the bar today?."

"No maa" said Purshottam, "give it away in charity", as Vakil Saab gave away two bundles of notes to charity too everyday.

Maa sat down near Purshottam and said "I have not been feeling well since a few days. I went to the Doctor but their medicines are not helping me."

Immediately Vakil Saab got up and made a small peg of country liquor and forced it down his mother's throat, in spite of her trying to say no. "You made me a sinner.. a sinner..." She mumbled. She was not happy. But now whenever Maa complained about her health, Vakil Saab gave her a peg to drink. His mother informed him after a month "Purshottam look at my feet, now I am so active, look how I have gained good health and strength." Vakil Saab laughed indulging his Mother and told her "Maa, Judge Saab's old medicine is curing you. You should have it everyday. All your ailments will run away. Maa retorted that Purshottam was pushing her towards the gates of hell in her old age. This is how they showed their love for each other.

One of those days Aadil and Gurudas went to Liban pub in the evening. It was beautiful and right on the shores of Marine Drive. They were dancing away and enjoying the music. Just then Bhau's son Rupesh entered the pub with his cronies and started throwing notes around the dancers. When Rupesh noticed Aadil and Gurudas, he started showing off. He gestured towards them and showed them the revolver hanging on his hip. Both of them were avoiding looking at him or his gestures and continued with their dancing. But Rupesh carried on showing off his revolver. Aadil went near Rupesh and said "Until now you have survived on what your father earned and his reputation. Try standing on your own feet and then show us the revolver." The moment Rupesh heard this his ego was hurt and he was wild with rage. He whipped out his revolver and aimed it at Aadil.

Aadil simply smiled and told him "Come on, let's play a game." and took out his revolver and took out all the bullets except one. He rolled the trigger and said "I have emptied five bullets and one is still in it. Put the barrel to your temple if you have the balls." Rupesh Kumar's ego was at stake. He was very badly shaken. Suddenly there was pin drop silence in the pub. People were just staring at Rupesh waiting for his reaction. Rupesh looked at everybody around the room and he realized that everybody was staring at him waiting for him to make the first move. There was no escape. Wiping his sweaty brow Rupesh mumbled "First you go." In a split second Aadil pointed the revolver on his temple and pulled the trigger. Everybody's hearts skipped a beat and the faint hearted turned away waiting for a splatter of blood. The silence was so heavy that you could hear all the hearts beating in rhythm. Luckily it was just the trigger noise. Everybody breathed a sigh of relief. Now it was Rupeshs' turn and he was looking at everybody around. He always depended on others to fight his battles so he waited for sometime and looked at the revolver and then his cronies. He soon realized that no one was coming to help him.

He was trying to gather courage but he could not. He turned pale, as if he had seen a ghost. He felt like death was looking at him right in the eye. He was feeling impotent in a room full of people staring at him. He started making excuses like "these sort of duels don't happen in a pub but in a battlefield." he slowly and slyly started shifting and in a few seconds he ran out of the pub with his cronies following him. In a split second Aadil had become a hero and Rupesh, a coward. The people watching this, rushed towards Aadil and hoisted him up in the air, celebrating his victory.

In any case people never held Bhau's family in high esteem. They were considered the scavengers of the corrupt world. They depended on the leftovers of other criminals.

As he left the pub, Rupesh was stung by the insult. Aadil had made him suffer, and he was ready to start plotting his revenge.

Vakil Saab had anyway made them suffer a loss of 25 crores, which was hurting them. Rupesh had occupied that land like a poisonous cobra for five years and he had to vacate the place and leave empty handed. He had not forgotten the loss of those 25 crores and this insult had added salt to the injury. Bhau and Rupesh were not on good terms either. They argued with each other every other day. The tree which yielded black money was soon drying up. The moment the cold cash stopped coming in, Bhau's respect in the house decreased. Nobody loved him, especially his wife. She only loved the cash he brought home. His situation at home was precarious, and that scared Bhau and made him insecure.

One morning, after a few days of this incident, Aadil's mobile phone rang. He could barely open his eyes. However, he answered the phone and it was Rampal at the other end. Aadil asked "Why are you calling me so early in the morning?" Rampal told him that a parcel had come for him from Gujarat and asked him to pick it up from Vakil Saab's godown. Aadil was wondering what it could be and rushed to the godown. When he got there he saw a broken van in the compound with a Gujarat licence plate.

Aadil opened the door of the van and found a man sitting inside, his hands were tied up and eyes blindfolded. Rampal informed Aadil "This is the man who had shot Vakil Saab. He was hiding in Ahmedabad. He has already confessed. You can hear him out too." Aadil removed his blindfold. The sudden bright light blinded him and he started blabbering away, as if on cue. "Please forgive me. Have mercy on me. My name is Masoom Ali Taili. I have a family waiting for me at home. Bhau had paid contract money to kill you. If I would have refused then Bhau's gang would have killed me. I am a well known shooter. He knew that my aim was good but that day a sadhu made me miss my target."

Aadil was shocked to hear the Sadhu's name being mentioned because that dark morning the place was completely deserted. The more Masoom Ali was narrating the incident, the more Aadil was sure that it was definitely the Sadhu from Kailash who had saved Vakil Saab's life. Aadil asked Masoom about the Mahatma's physical appearance and he was very sure that it was definitely Mahatmaji. He could have killed Masoom Ali but he took him to Vakil Saab. Vakil Saab had faith in the Indian Constitution so he handed him over to the police. Masoom's confession made it to all the Maharashtra and Gujarat newspapers. It was in the headlines the next day and it turned out to be quite a furore in the criminal world. The whole incident was served to the readers on a platter with salt and pepper by the media.

Vakil Saab was made a hero by the editor of 'Kal Ka Bharat' (a local publication). His name was mentioned in the editorial as a saviour (messiah) of victims. After a sensational confession given by Masoom Ali, Bhau was dragged in the middle of the night and put behind bars. Rupesh Kumar was dumbfounded when he heard about his father's arrest. He had never thought that the police will track them down to their gang's hideout. The next day he sounded a little over confident and foolish when he talked to the media. "I will not let them keep my father in jail for even one night. I challenge them. My father has been trapped by the Vakil.. I will bring the whole city to a halt if they don't release him immediately." he ranted but nothing happened and people were making fun of his futile banter. Rupesh went to bail his father out with a horde of lawyers but he failed to do so as Vakil Saab had cleverly laid a very smart legal trap that put Bhau in the lowest category of criminals. Rupesh Kumar's antics had now made his prestige bite the dust. Earlier Bhau had dominated the whole of Maharashtra. He could initiate riots anytime he wanted and stop them anytime he wanted. He was held in great esteem in the higher society but today none of the political parties were ready to support him. Rupesh Kumar begged at every doorstep but nobody heard his pleas. One of the reasons for that was that Rupesh himself as had often shifted his alliance from one Party to another for small but selfish reasons. He continued behaving rashly like a roadside romeo and Bhau continued to ignore his misbehaviour. That turned out to be Bhau's biggest mistake. Politicians whose offices Bhau often visited as a respected citizen were avoiding him like the plague. Bhau was having the regular jail food from a dirty aluminium vessel sitting on the floor behind bars and was thinking about Rampal. Rampal was his last ray of hope. Rampal was a sentimental man and he used his heart more than his head. When Rampal was working for him Bhau always took advantage of his innocence and it was always undue advantage. But now Rampal's nature had changed completely and Bhau did not know that. Bhau sent a message that he wanted to meet Rampal. Whenever Bhau was plunged into a problem, it was Rampal who always pulled him out of doldrums.

When Bhau met Rampal in jail, old memories enveloped them like a gust of wind. Rampal had committed two murders for Bhau at a snap of a finger. One was sugar mafia Mohan Shikare and the second was sand mafia Eknath Koli. Both were very powerful mafias. The police also thought twice before putting their foot in their area. A few years back a brave Inspector called Diwakar had dared to enter their citadel. He had to manoeuvre through narrow lanes before he could make it to his small little room. The moment they saw him in the lane somebody threw a big chunk of metal on him from above. Diwaker died instantly. This murderous attack was made out to be a mere accident by the white collar workers and the case was closed. The police were very upset that a brave person like Diwaker was killed by a mere hooligan.

Bhau had dared to venture where no one dared. One day a drunk Bhau was ranting away, "Mohan Shikare and Eknath Koli, both are my enemies… they are my biggest obstacles. If we manage to remove them then I will be the biggest Don (Bhai) of Maharashtra. Mohan Shikare's sugar mill is my weakness. I want my name on that sugar mill board." Rampal, who was sitting beside him, was listening to Bhau's banter. Bhau asked Rampal casually "Ramya you are like a second son to me. Will you fulfill my dream? " Rampal said "I do not understand what you want from me." Bhau tried to ensnare Rampal in his web of words. Even though he was drunk, he knew exactly what he was saying. Bhau told him "Ramya you are my son. I have taken care of you since you were a baby. I have fed you like I would have fed my child. I have been like a father to you. I know for a fact that you are not a traitor. If I am like your father then it is your duty to fulfill my dreams and you owe it to me. "Rampal was overcome with emotions listening to Bhau's continuous chatter. Bhau took advantage of this and tried to make him more sentimental. Bhau told him "Ramya you tell me one thing. If your very own Father was alive you definitely would have tried to fulfill his dreams(wishes)?. After listening to Bhau, Rampal could not think straight. He was always a gullible man with a big soft heart. He could be easily manipulated. With Bhau's emotional blackmail Rampal was being tossed around in the flow of emotions which he himself could not understand. Bhau could not help but notice that Rampal's was melting like wax in front of the fire he was igniting.. This was the correct time to temper the sizzling hot metal in Rampal's steel like heart. Bhau added "Ramya, do let me know if you need something. I promise, you will never return empty handed." He finished the conversation while putting his hand on his head and adding" Just remove Eknath Koli and Mohan Shikare from my road to success, my son"

That was why Rampal was sentenced for life, for Mohan Shikare and Eknath Koli's murder. After the job was done Bhau started ignoring Rampal which ended in Rampal's lawful arrest. The remaining amount of what Rampal had earned on that job, he used to help Vakil Saab by making Rupesh vacate the plot and made a place for himself in the Vakil gang. He was edging his way out of the Bhau gang. Now he had learnt to take advantage of people and he was biding his time.

For a moment or two Bhau silently looked at Rampal. He realized that Rampal had changed and he won't be able to use him like he had in the past. Rampal broke the silence and said "Please tell me why have you called me." A tired Bhau replied slowly, "You know why Rampal." Rampal informed him that his Parole time was over. He said "In two days time I will be back in Yerwada Jail. I cannot help you in any way." When Bhau heard him he immediately said "You can do everything. I am feeling suffocated here. I suffer from high blood pressure and diabetes." Rampal replied like a seasoned player "Freedom from jail. That is what you want. You know the price

Bhau Saab. I will talk with Vakil Saab. I will. But Bhau Saab, you know Vakil Saab has his own price and his own principles to make a deal. Maybe this deal may turn out to be a little costly for you."

Rampal was dealing with Bhau like a shrewd money lender would with his dealers fleecing him of everything. Bhau noticed the change in Rampal but he desperately wanted to keep the Sugar mill. He needed the mill like he needed a spine in his back and Rampal wanted to break his back by taking the Sugar Mill away from him. Bhau felt powerless. His silence had said everything. It said that he had surrendered to Rampal's pressure tactics.

That very night Rampal met Vakil Saab. He approached him as a mediator from Bhau's side. Vakil Saab heard what he had to say and sat quietly for some time. He gave the matter a good thought and asked Rampal to decide the price. He knew well that Rampal had turned into a good deal maker. He was not the innocent Rampal, Bhau once knew. The reason for this transformation was Bhau himself. Bhau had usurped Mohan Shikare's Sugar mill by getting him murdered by Rampal and he had not forgotten that fact. Bhau was under Rampal's obligation for the ownership of the Sugar Mill. Rampal contemplated the situation. If Vakil Saab will get the ownership of the Sugar mill then Bhau will have to bow down to him. That is exactly what Rampal wanted. Rampal spun a web of malice and it had Vakil Saab's stamp of agreement on it. He went to meet Bhau in jail again. When Bhau heard about the Sugar mill he was aghast. Beads of perspiration trickled down his forehead. His mental state was very obvious. It seemed as if his blood pressure had shot high. Rampal was enjoying the fact that Bhau was very upset. Bhau was behaving as if he had actually toiled day and night for that mill and he owned the mill. He realized he was getting old now. He had always been the bread earner of the family and his wife and children never loved him. They only loved the money he brought home. They would never help him get out of jail. He soon accepted defeat and closed the deal on Rampal's terms. The next day Vakil Saab changed his game strategy for the case and Bhau was free. Now Bhau was penniless. He was neither respected in his home nor outside his home. After losing the Sugar mill the situation at home was like a battlefield of Mahabharat. Bhau had been blinded by his love for his son like Dhrutarashtra and was repenting it. He had planted a babool tree with thorns, how could he expect a sweet fruit from it. Now Bhau had turned into a dried tree which did not give a fruit nor any shade to a tired traveller. He was inching towards his end. He was reaping what he had sowed. That was God's will.

In the meanwhile it was celebration time for Rampal at the Sonali Bar. Rampal's accomplishments were the talk of the town. Rampal was now considered an equal partner in Vakil Saab's gang. He was as big a part of the Vakil gang as Aadil and Gurpal. This was a big victory for Rampal. He always proved to be lucky for Vakil Saab in all his ventures.

In the midst of all this celebration, a very haggard old man entered the bar. His white beard looked untrimmed. His face mirrored a lot of hurt and anguish. His eyes were pouring out his expectations from Vakil Saab. He told Aadil that he wanted to talk with Vakil Saab. He said "I need to talk urgently." Aadil could sense his urgency. Hearing this Vakil Saab approached him and the old man immediately said "I am Mansukhlal Khandwala. I had made a deal for a bungalow for four crores. I have given fifty lakhs as token money to the owner. The balance amount including the loan was to be paid within thirty days. Because of the Bank's careless attitude I was late by one day. Now the owner of the Bungalow is neither returning my fifty lakhs nor is he processing the deal further." Vakil Saab glanced at Aadil for a split second and said "You should go to the police." Mansukhlal said" I am coming to you straight from the police station. They saw my 'Memorandum of Understanding' and said that I cannot do anything about it. It has been clearly mentioned in the Memorandum of Understanding that the payment should be done within thirty days." Vakil Saab took the Memorandum and read it. It was very clear. Mansukhlal had agreed to all the terms and conditions and had signed it too. Vakil Saab thought that usually in such matters a forty day breather is always given. Aadil said "Vakil Saab, I had heard of a similar matter a few months ago." Vakil Saab read the Memorandum again and he suddenly noticed one of the conditions. It was a very strange condition. The loan was to be procured only from IDIC Bank. Vakil Saab asked the old man why he had paid such a big amount as token money. Mansukhlal replied "One of the conditions was that the token money has to be at least fifty lakhs. Vakil Saab understood the case immediately. They had created a web of clever words and the demand for fifty lakhs as token money was also strange. The cheque being issued late was also unusual. Vakil Saab read aloud the name of the owner, "Natwarlal Mahodiya." Aadil suddenly remembered something. He said "Vakil Saab, he is Gulabdas Bhati's son-in-law. The same Gulabdas who had sold his land to our builder Prakash Nainani. The same Gulabdas had instigated Bhau's son Rupesh to occupy the land. Gulabdas Bhati has been deceiving many builders and double crossing them in the game."

Gulabdas would buy land at a cheaper rate than the market price and sell it at an even cheaper rate to the builders. After this Bhau's son would forcibly occupy the land. After all this Bhati would act as the mediator and a big amount was squeezed out from the buyer. At the end of the day when the Builder would finally sit down to do the total his mind would be blown away. The price of the land would cost him almost double the actual price.

Gulabdas Bhati and his son-in-law Natwarlal were good friends with Bhau. Vakil Saab understood that this fraud was a deliberate pre-planned thing.

Vakil Saab took the Broker's name and contact details from Mansukhlal. Vakil Saab was now very excited about the case. He wanted to enjoy this game with Bhau and he wanted an in depth understanding of this case of fraud. He decided to check exactly how many people this gang had fleeced. His mind had started ticking away like a clock.

The next day Aadil called the Broker to Vakil Saab's godown. Broker Baban was very excited at this prospect. He reached the godown with his mind brimming with ideas to put forth. The moment he reached, he met Aadil and put all his cards on the table and asked "How much do you want to invest Saab. I have a budget from twenty five lakhs to twenty five crores."

Aadil was quietly listening to the Broker. Baban was talking like a typical broker. He continued "The under construction project will give you a big profit Saab." Aadil said "Why don't you eat something first." The next instant Aadil's assistants, who were waiting for a cue, started beating up Baban. He was petrified by this sudden assault. He could not understand why they were hitting him. He started begging for his life with folded hands and asked "What did I do Saab. Did I do something wrong? Please don't hit me. Don't hit me… Please…" That did not stop them from what they were doing. They knew that it was necessary to hit mercilessly until Baban felt the terror in every nerve of his body. After a lot of thrashing Aadil told them to stop. Baban was on his knees and was blabbering away "Please let me go." Just then Vakil Saab entered and took his seat with a swish of his chair.. The moment Baban saw him he started shaking like a leaf. Aadil said sarcastically "Now that you have eaten well, let us talk about business." He added "Now start talking…after taking twenty five lakh as token money then insisting on taking a loan from IDIC bank, then delaying the cheque for one day what happened?. You better explain all this in a very simple way so we understand easily." It did not take long for Baban to understand that all the thrashing he received was for Natwarlal's case. In a split second Babban was on his knees, shaking and blurting out every thing like a scared crow. It sounded like a story right out of a movie. Babban said "the first thing we did was we lured him with a low price of the land, then we said we need a big amount of token money and it was written in the MOU that the loan was to be taken from only IDIC bank. After the token was taken, the bank lobby and I would get twenty percent of the price which is fifteen lakhs. The bank manager Hari Shirsat would immediately approve the bank loan. Eligible for loan sanction letter was then signed and given to the buyer so that the person taking the loan was convinced and sure about getting the loan. After the cheque was ready the Operation Manager would sign the cheque, which left only the bank manager's signature. On the thirtieth day the manager would complain about chest pains and get admitted in Nirmala Nursing Home. By doing this the cheque would be late by one day. Shirsat would enjoy his stay at the hospital drinking sips of beer while Doctor Patil would be very pleased with the mediclaim money he would get. The moment the cheque was delayed, according to the Memorandum of Understanding, Natwarlal would get his share of the token money. All of us would share the money. I would get five lakhs, the bank manager Hari Shirsat would get his share of five lakhs and the Operation manager Diwaker would get his share of five lakhs." Babban was still on his knees and ranting "I have told you the whole truth and nothing but the truth, can I go now?"

A few moments of silence prevailed in the godown. Vakil Saab lit his cigarette, took a puff, filled his lungs with the smoke and looked at Aadil and blew out rings of smoke. Aadil asked Babban "how many people are there in your family?" The moment he heard this, Babban was soaked to his skin in perspiration. He did not utter a single word. Vakil Saab pierced him with his gaze and Babban started talking, "two kids, one wife and an old ailing mother" Aadil immediately asked him, "Babban if you die in a road accident then what will happen to your family? They will end up on the road." Babban started wiping his tears and perspiration too, you could see the fear in his eyes. He grabbed Vakil Saab's legs and started begging "Please don't do anything like that Saab, please forgive me. I will give you my share of five lakhs. Vakill Saab took a big puff and tapped the ash from his cigarette and said "You don't need to return the cash. You continue doing what you have been doing all this time." Babban was dumbfounded. He could not understand what Vakil Saab was trying to tell him. So Aadil explained "You change the cost of the Bungalow from five crores to two crores and take one crore as token money. According to your previous conditions, there will be a loan of fifty lakhs from IDIC bank. We will do the payment of fifty lakhs by Demand Draft, and we will continue doing the rest of the procedure step by step and no one will even get a whiff of the whole thing. Babban was still holding on to Vakil Saab's feet. He said "I will do what you tell me to do. I will obey every order." Adil said "One crore token money, Fifty lakh loan amount and fifty by demand draft. You dare not disclose this to anyone. Just keep your mouth shut."

When Babban left Vakil Saab's godown he weighed down with fear. He had to drag his feet while walking out of the godown. He could not sleep the entire night. He felt as if he was sleeping on a slab of ice and his bones were creaking and breaking. Though Babban was terrified he hid this feeling and reached Natwarlal's house with a fresh and smiling face. Natwarlal was happy to see Babban approaching him. He thought to himself "I will be getting fifty lakhs again." Natwarlal's greedy wife immediately put a spread of snacks in front of Babban.

Babban started talking as if he was a robot. He said "Natwarlalji this time the token money is double." Natwarlal asked "Why?" Babban said "I tried to convince one party, but this time the price of the bungalow is two crores. The moment he heard this Natwarlal looked at his wife and both were silent for some time. Babban was feeling very uneasy.

Natwarlal's greedy wife was keen to get the money and said "It's fine. Why should we be worried? We are not going to sell the bungalow anyway." She sat beside Natwarlal and continued "Sweetheart, this time the token money is double, so we can make a trip to Dubai the moment we get the cash in hand." Both the husband and wife were almost drowning in the river of greed. It was like how a fox looks at a honeycomb full of honey. The moment they heard about the two crores both of them agreed immediately. Babban then went to tell them "Natwarlalji, this time my share would be thirty lakhs and yours will be seventy. This time the token money is doubled." Natwarlal agreed with Babban and asked him when was he going to bring the buyer.

Babban replied "Very soon. Bhabhiji you start packing for Dubai." And he left.

Immediately he went to Vakil Saab's godown. Vakil Saab had fixed up a deal with Mansukhlal for the bungalow. Mansukhlal would make a profit of one crore and he would get his fifty lakh back too. Aadil threw the MOU towards Babban and said "Read this. All the conditions are in Natwarlal's favour." The bungalow was to be bought in Mansukhlal's wife's name. She was Sushila Khandwala. Vakil Saab had put the price of the Bunglow at four crores and Mansukhlal had agreed. Two crore was to be given to Vakil Saab after the possession. Sushila came to see the bungalow with Babban with her saree pallu draped over her head looking like a typical housewife. The moment Natwarlal heard the name Khandwala he said "She is also Khandwala?" Babban took Natwarlal in a corner and told him "Why are you spoiling the deal? Why are you digging your own grave? If they have any doubts they will cancel the whole deal. Just sit quietly and take the one crore as token money. It seems you do have some connection with the Khandwala name." The moment the deal was done Natwarlal received a cheque of one crore. Natwarlal was dancing with joy with the cheque in hand. The next day Natwarlal gave the thirty lakhs to Babban so that the whole drama could start. This time around everybody received double money so everybody was very happy.

The Bank manager immediately verified all the papers and stamped the eligibility letter. Within a few days the bank approval letter was sent too, so the party would be convinced that the process had started. Babban kept Aadil posted on all the events.

Now Natwarlal's role in the whole drama was over. The husband and wife left for their Dubai trip with seventy lakhs in hand. The whole amount was being splurged on their lavish holiday and shopping. They didn't care about expenses as cash was flowing like a river. The cheque was ready and the final days were approaching. The Operation Manager signed the cheque. Now only the Bank Manager Hari Shirsat's sign was pending. On the thirtieth day Sushila Khandwala finally went to the Bank to receive the cheque. She was told that Hari was admitted in the Nirmal Nursing home as he had complained about chest pains. He had been put in the ICU under observation by the doctors.

The cheque could not be deposited without Hari Shirsat's signature. Sushila explained to the bank staff "My deal will be canceled if I don't give the cheque to the Bungalow owner today. According to the terms and conditions if I don't give the cheque today I will lose all the token money. I will lose One crore and it will go to the owner. My life will be ruined." The Bank staff didn't care about any of that. They didn't care whether Sushila Khandwala's life was ruined. The whole staff had received their share of the money. Sushila Khandwala was complaining, but no one bothered to give her a ear. Sushila too knew that they would not listen. She wrote a letter and said "Please give me the reason for the delay of the cheque in writing. The bank staff immediately gave her the letter stating, "Last night Hari Shirsat developed chest pains and he was admitted in Nirmal Nursing Home. Doctor has given 48 hours. He is under observation in ICU." The moment she got the letter in hand Sushila forwarded the letter via Whatsapp to Vakil Saab. He read the letter and told Aadil "Today will be the climax of this whole drama." Hari Shirsat was enjoying his beer on the hospital bed. He was supposed to be in the hospital according to their plan so that a very valid excuse could be given. Fake ECG, fake cardiogram, fake prescriptions, everything was fake. The fake reports Doctor Patil had completed were with a lot of honesty and he had received a fat sum of money for it, including the cash from the Mediclaim. Sushila had registered her entry in the bank register. On the other hand Vakil Saab had put together a team which had a Government Doctor and a local police Inspector. Equipped with a video camera Vakil Saab along with the Doctor and the Inspector raided Nirmal Nursing Home. Bank Manager Shirsat was playing a video game on his mobile in a private room oblivious of the situation. There was a glass of beer on the side table for him. While the raid with a video camera created a commotion in the nursing home. The nurses started running helter-skelter. Even the ward boys tried to stop them but they were unsuccessful. The Hawaldar accompanying them entered and grabbed Hari Shirsat's mobile. A scared Doctor Patil entered the room but his mobile was also confiscated.

The Government Doctor started checking Shirsat. Blood pressure was normal, ECG was normal, the Cardiogram report was also normal. Doctor Patil and Shirsat were caught in a bad situation. Both were on their knees, begging for life from Vakil Saab.

Vakil Saab's modus operandi was different from others. He worked in tandem with the law and destroyed the opposite camp completely.

Doctor Patil looked at Vakil Saab and said, "We can sit in this room and you hear us out." Vakil Saab looked at Aadil and he understood that this was the moment they were waiting for. Vakil Saab, Aadil, Doctor Patil and Hari Shirsat sat down for a meeting. After a few moments of silence Doctor Patil asked "Now tell us Vakil Saab what is your demand." Aadil replied "You will give one crore and Hari Shirsatji will give fifty lakhs. Both of them turned and looked at each other. Patil was shocked. "That is a big amount," he said. Aadil looked at Vakil Saab. Vakil Saab silently put a cigarette to his lips, Aadil bent forward to light his cigarette. Vakil Saab took a big puff and blew smoke rings in the air as usual. Aadil looked at Doctor Patil and said "Doctor Saab you need to pay for your deeds. You have cheated and digested crores from the Insurance Company. You are worshipped in the society like a God. If the people got to know about your exploits, you will turn into a devil in a split second. Your actions show that you are a devil and you love money. If we tell everyone about your misdeeds, your name will be slandered. A 'fox in sheep's clothing', that is how your name will be mentioned in tomorrow's headlines and you will be facing long lonely nights in prison." The moment Doctor Patil heard all this, he said "I'll do it." He was so scared that he started wiping his perspiring forehead and added, "Where should I deliver the cash?" Aadil called Gurudas and made the doctor talk to him. Hari Shirsat too agreed to the deal immediately, as he was scared for his life. After receiving one crore from Doctor Patil and fifty lakhs From Shirsat, Aadil messaged Gurudas. The moment they received the cash they deleted the recorded video.

However there was still an important bit missing in the big picture and that was Hari Shirsat's signature on the cheque. Hari called up the Bank. Diwaker reached the Nursing Home with the cheque. Hari signed the cheque for the last time. But the job was not done yet. They were yet to go to Natwarlal's house and give the cheque to him through Sushila Khandwala before midnight, with Shirsat and Vakil Saab as witnesses so that Sushila could be the new owner.

It was almost six in the evening. Everybody left for Natwarlal's house. Just then Shirsat said "I want to go to the washroom." His mobile was with the hawaldar, but Shirsat managed to warn Natwarlal with a hidden mobile so that he would leave his house for one night.

Natwarlal was tense the moment he received the message. He realized he had got entangled in his own web of lies. When his wife knew what had happened she was very depressed. She regretted spending so much money in Dubai. A bungalow worth five crores was going to be sold for only two crores. The whole household was in a tizzy. They had to leave the house before Sushila Khandwala and Vakil Saab arrived with their entourage. Natwarlal immediately packed a few clothes for him and his wife and quickly took out his car. They even asked their cook to sit with them in the car and left for an unknown location.

Vakil Saab was on the way with his full team in his big Innova car. Bank manager Hari Shirsat, Broker Babban, Sushila and her husband Mansukhlal Khandwala and the local police. He wanted to handover the cheque to Natwarlal with all these people as witnesses so that the payment would be done as per his conditions. Aadil sped the car. Hari Shirsat was uneasy. He said "Natwarlal's house is in Mumbai then why are we going in a different direction?" While saying this he looked at Babban. Babban too was confused but both of them were too scared to ask Vakil Saab anything. The car was running at full speed. When they reached Panvel, Shirsat finally asked "Vakil Saab, please tell me where we are headed." Aadil replied "We are going to meet Natwarlal." Hari said "Natwarlal's house is in Mumbai." To which Vakil Saab replied "Natwarlal and his wife left Mumbai the moment they read your message." Aadil took out a mobile from his pocket while driving and said "This is the same mobile you had used to send the message. Right?" The moment Shirsat heard this he started sweating. He was embarrassed of his own treachery. Aadil said "Hariji, let me tell you one thing. Treachery flows in your blood and it is impossible to throw it out of your system."

Hari's face went pale with fear and embarrassment. Finally after a drive of four hours they reached Lonavala's Bella Resort. When Vakil Saab looked at his watch it was eleven in the night. They had one hour left to close the deal, according to the contract. Vakil Saab had to overturn the plot in that one hour.

Aadil inquired at the reception for Natwarlal's room. The Butler showed them to the room. Aadil knocked on the door and said "Room service."

Natwarlal's beautiful wife opened the door. And there stood Sushila Khandwala at the door, with a cheque in her hand. Shirsat, Babban and a police Inspector were also standing right behind her. Natwarlal had just reached the room but little did he know that a big catastrophe had followed him. The moment he saw Mansukhlal Khandwala standing behind them he realized that his game was over.

Sushila Khandwala broke the silence, "According to the Memorandum of Understanding I had to pay you fifty lakhs in cash and fifty lakhs as Demand Draft. Here is your fifty lakhs in cash and fifty as DD. Please take this and sign the received paper. Natwarlal did not know how to react. He looked at Babban, but Babban looked away. The Bank manager's face went pale like a ghost's. He just stood there with his head down.

Natwarlal and his wife looked at each other. They were confused and shaken. They realised they did not have an option. According to the MOU, today was the last date and a few minutes were still left of the last hour. Natwarlal could not deny it with so many people looking at him. Natwarlal started signing like a robot on the cash and cheque received paper. Vakil Saab made Babban and Shirsat sign as witnesses. Vakil Saab also made Natwarlal's wife sign and put a thumb impression. Sushila Khandwala received the keys to the Bungalow.

The whole team started congratulating each other and then left the hotel. Natwarlal and his wife could not wrap their heads around what had just happened. They were at a loss. It felt as if a strong gust of wind had come and taken away everything in its way.

The husband and wife were trapped in their own web of lies. They had only one crore seventy lakhs in hand for a bungalow worth five crores. Thirty lakhs were already given to Babban and the Bank Manager. They felt like they had lost everything. As if they were homeless in their own country.

The next day Mansukhlal came to Vakil Saab's office with two crores in cash and a box of sweets. The deal had turned out to be very profitable. Two crores were from Mansukhlal Khandwala, one crore from Doctor Patil and fifty lakhs from the Bank manager, Hari Shirsat. They had a total of three crores and fifty lakhs lying on the table. Before distributing the cash to everybody Vakil Saab kept twenty lakhs aside. Aadil and Gurudas saw this and Vakil Saab instantly knew what they were thinking. He looked at them and said, "This is Rampal's share. Now he too is a part of our gang."

Rampal was spending the remaining days of imprisonment in Yerwada Jail peacefully. He had sadly but surely realized that he finally had someone to support him. He had made a few good connections in jail on account of his good behaviour. His willingness to do anything for his friends was hugely appreciated. The police were using him and he was aware of the fact that he was being used as a pawn in Bhau's game.

Vakil Saab reigned all over Mumbai now. Ever since the day Vakil Saab had grabbed the Sugar Mill from Bhau, word on the street was that, "Vakil Saab is living like a conniving fox under his legal garb mingling with the posh and aristocratic." But such statements never bothered Vakil Saab. Black money earnings continued to grow and were weighing him down but Vakil Saab's brain always worked like a true blue blooded Gujarati. He would invest a part of his earnings in multinational companies and the remaining he would put into film-making.

After the Bungalow episode, the grieving Gulabdas Bhati, Natwarlal and his beautiful wife went to Bhau's house. The husband and wife had been out of their mind after they lost such a prime property in just two crores. Till now Gulabdas Bhati had always depended on Bhau and Rupesh for all his illegal businesses. Whenever he was trapped in a bad situation he would beg Bhau to help him. Though Gulabdas knew that Vakil Saab and Bhau did not get along, what he did not know was that Bhau was like an empty vessel now and he could not help anyone. Bhau listened to Natwarlal's side of the story; of how Vakil Saab had played his shrewd game and trapped them. Listening to this story made Bhau sweaty and nervous. But he did not show it.

Natwarlal was pleading with him, "Bhau Saab, please help me! We are on the streets and all the money's gone." Bhau was thinking that Vakil Saab had spoiled the show so badly that nothing could be done to salvage it. Bhau did not want to add to his problems. He simply got up and left the room. Gulabdas and Natwarlal just stared at his receding back. Bhau's exit made it very clear that Bhau was not interested in being involved with anything to do with Vakil Saab anymore.

Natwarlal's wife was sobbing inconsolably and was not in her senses. Her saree was slipping down as she tried to wipe her tears. Her beautiful navel, peeping enticingly from under her saree. Rupesh, being the typical playboy, couldn't take his eyes off her slim and shiny waist. He was staring at her navel and her heaving bosom with lustful eyes. A woman's navel was his weak point and it turned him into a wild animal.

After leaving the room, Bhau sat down to have a drink in a closed room. He was unaware of the things going on outside. He was very unhappy and disturbed he had lost the Sugar mill and with it his prestige too. He was also facing losses every day because of this. There was a storm raging in his heart. He was looking forward to a final fight with Vakil Saab. But he did not want anybody's help. Bhau was almost sixty and he had lost almost everything he had worked hard for his entire life. He looked at his mother's photograph hanging on the wall and closed his eyes. He imagined he was in his mother's lap. When he closed his eyes, memories of his childhood flooded his mind and suddenly he was at peace with the whole world.

His mind took him in a flashback. He remembered how he was a young boy in the seventies. He studied in a Municipal school. He lost his father, Laxman in a train accident when he was six. But his mother Kashibai never accepted it. She always said that the Mill Union Leader had cheated and killed him. His father was a very hard working man. When the Union announced the closure of the mill, Laxman visited everybody's houses and told them "Arre the Mill is like our Mother. She gives us food.

If the mill is closed down, all of us will go hungry. Do not listen to what the union is saying."

The union did not like what Laxman said. He was like a pebble in the shoe, pinching them every step of the way. They wanted him out of their way and he eventually died in a train accident. People forgot about Laxman as days passed by, but Kashibai could not. She always said that the Union killed her husband but nobody listened to her nor did anyone believe her.

Kashibai was an expert cook and prepared delicious meals. She provided tiffin service to people but never worried about profit or loss. She took joy in the fact that they enjoyed her food and blessed her. Bhau was a kid then and he would deliver the tiffins to different houses.

During this time, a new theatre called Ocean Talkies was built in Ghatkopar. The first film released was 'Blackmail', a big hit at that time. Bhau, who was fourteen then, started selling the tickets in black.

Chhota Rajan from Tilak Nagar, Chembur was also murdered in those years. During his funeral procession all the roads from Tilak Nagar to Rajawadi in Ghatkopar were full of people. He had a huge following. This made a big impression on fourteen year old Bhau. He decided he will have a gang of his own and will be a don like Rajan. He selected a few boys of his age and they started selling tickets in black in all the theatres in Ghatkopar.

This was his first step towards all the wrong things in his life. He would deliver liquor in tyre tubes to all the illegal bars from the Country liquor distillery, which was in the Godrej Creek at Vikhroli. Now he was unstoppable. As his business progressed a boy named Chandu from his group started a separate gang and started selling black tickets in the same theatres. Bhau did not like this. He did not like anybody rising to a level above him. He knew that if he would bow down to Chandu, he would never become a Chota Rajan.

He called Chandu to meet him at Ocean Talkies and very effortlessly killed him with his knife. Blood spattered all over the theatre. People who witnessed this, started screaming and shouting. Seeing all hell break loose, Bhau ran from there like a scared rabbit with his hands red with Chandu's blood. Police arrived on the spot after a while and rushed Chandu to Rajawadi Hospital. If he was taken to the hospital earlier, Chandu could have survived.

Bhau rushed to meet his mother like a scared child. He blurted everything that had happened. When his mother heard everything, she thrashed Bhau mercilessly. But after all she was a Mother. She feared that if he would go to jail, he would never get out of there and she would be left alone forever. She took him where she could save him.

In those days there was a blind Don in Ghatkopar named Bhupat Singh Rathod. People were afraid of him and his presence dominated the crime scene of Ghatkopar. At the time Ghatkopar was flooded with spunky Gujaratis who were well known for their business sense. Nobody dared to cross paths with them, especially with people from Saurashtra.

Bhau's mother took him to meet Bhupat singh and said, "Sheth, have mercy on me, he is my only child and he is only fourteen. Only you can save him, Sheth."

Bhupat Singh observed Bhau for a long time through his fancy sunglasses. After this sentimental outpour, the love of a mother had done the trick. Bhupat Singh said "Kashibai, your son will be safe with me."

When the case came up in the court, nobody appeared as a witness out of fear and the case was dismissed. Bhupat Singh also gave Bhau's Mother one lakh as charity.

Bhupat Singh took Bhau under his wings which emboldened him further. He started behaving in a high-handed manner at Ocean Talkies. The Manager and the owner were now scared of Bhau. A few boys from Chembur and Vikhroli also started selling tickets illegally. All the boys had a gang of their own. The boy gangs had a tussle regularly. Altercations between them often ended in knife fights. In a period of two years, seven murders were committed in that area.

Under normal circumstances that was a huge number. Eventually the screening license of Ocean Talkies was cancelled and now Bhau started scouring other means and options. He did not want to waste his precious time on petty fights.

Ramju Ali Kachhi staying on Sixty Feet Road in Ambika Bhuvan was a Muslim who considered himself a lookalike of Rajkumar, the Film star. He actually did look like him too. He had the same hairstyle, the same swag, the same walk and the same style of wearing white shoes. People from far off places came just to have a look at him. Ramju Ali had his connections with fashion and with crime too. Amongst these connections there was a connection with the fashion savvy Moti Lalwani. He too lived in Ghatkopar in a small lane called Sindhu Wadi.

Lalwani smuggled Electronics and Textile Materials under the guise of a job in the Dockyard. He was well known from Dockyard Road to Ulhasnagar for dealing in illegal goods due to which he kept good relations with the police department.

As Ramju Ali and Moti Lalwani were the two sides of the same coin in the world of crime, they would often meet at a small Irani Hotel for Bun maska and the famous Irani tea. They had the same affinity towards music so they would listen to songs played on the Jukebox. The Jukebox played music with just a twenty five paisa coin, which was a very small amount in those days. This tea and music party lasted for a long time. During one such evening Lalvani mentioned that he was getting old and weak and he needed a smart, young and daring boy to assist him.

When Ramju Ali saw Bhau he remembered Lalwani's words and fixed a meeting between the two of them at the same Irani Hotel. When Bhau met Lalwani for the first time he was very impressed with his personality. Lalwani was wearing a white shirt and white pants with a thick gold chain around his neck and a costly watch on his wrist. Bhau was so impressed that he decided that one day he too would own a gold chain and a costly watch like him and become famous. Bhau was desperate to earn money and fame and did not care how he got it. This desperation always damaged his reputation and it affected his future decisions too.

Now that Bhau had started working with Lalwani, he accompanied him to work too. Lalwani would take him to the Ballard Pier in his big Ambassador car. Bhau too was learning the tricks of the trade with complete faith. As time passed Bhau had learnt everything which was necessary from Lalwani.

Lalwani's old age was slowing him down and he could not do his business with the vigour and vitality which was needed. He also realized that Bhau had moved ahead of him and reached a higher level. Following Lalwani's footsteps Bhau had also started smuggling. Double Ghoda (double horse), Bosky material and white triple Panja Kati material was very much in demand in those days. He would pick up the material straight from the dock and supply it all over Mumbai and mint money.

Bhau had asked his mother to stop cooking for others. He bought a new car, a Premier Padmini, and took his mother for a tour of Mumbai. He would tell his mother "Maa, none of those Red Boxes anymore (the red BEST buses were called red boxes in the seventies). Now you can use this new Fiat car, whenever you want to go out."

Bhau always loved to do things for his Mother. He took his mother to Pandharpur, a village where all old people would go for pilgrimage. When the mother realized that Bhau had started earning well she got him married to Surekha from Satara. Within a year both of them were parents to a healthy baby boy. He was no more the same Bhau he used to be. He had become a big businessman with a lavish lifestyle. He had built a huge bungalow too.

Soon they had another addition to the family. During one of the visits to her mother, his wife Surekha came back with an orphan boy with her. Bhau asked her who he was. Surekha said that he was an orphan and he could stay in the house and help her with the housework. Everybody in the village called him Ramya. Ramya fitted in their house very easily. He started helping everyone with the household chores. Kashi bai loved him immensely and he too was very happy to receive this motherly love from her, which he badly missed. He tended to every little need. He would massage Kashi bai's hands and feet at night when she was tired. For Bhau he would pour soda and ice in his drink every night. Ramya was like a family member now.

Surekha too called him sometimes to massage her feet at night. This irritated Bhau but Surekha believed that he was just a kid and he did not have any vulgar thoughts in his mind.

Whenever Ramya had free time on his hands he would stand on the balcony and watch the kids playing on the street. Kashibai would see him looking at the children with a longing in his eyes to go and play. She would tell him, "You can go down and play Ramya." Ramya would run down and start playing with the other children. But as he started growing up, his innocence was left behind and he started to walk on the road leading to the world of crime. He never had the time to think about himself. He would just take orders from Bhai like a slave. Bhau thought that Ramya would be his slave forever. But although he was tied down in the shackles of slavery, he turned out to be a dreaded criminal. Bhau made him commit crimes for his own selfish reasons.

That innocent boy Ramya had become Rampal now. He rebelled and broke free from the slavery he was tied down to. He fled from the clutches of Bhau to the warm embrace of Vakil Saab. This was a big loss for Bhau. Vakil Saab had turned Rampal into a well known "goonda" of Ghatkopar again. He had started to deal in drugs now, for which he was not very happy. He did not enjoy working under anyone or anybody ruling over him.

Bhau's mind was racing with thoughts. There was a storm stirring inside his heart. He picked up his glass of whiskey and smashed it down in a wild rage. Rupesh Kumar ran to the room when he heard the noise of breaking glass. Bhau was sloshed with too much whiskey. Gulabdas Bhati followed Rupesh. Rupesh supported his father and helped him lay down on the bed. Gulabdas left Bhau's house with his daughter and son-in-law. The ship was sinking with no shoreline visible.

Around the same time Vakil Saab received an invitation and he asked Aadil to read the printed card. Aadil read it and awkwardly returned it to Vakil Saab before walking out of the room. Reshma Billi's album was going to be released on the 21st of that month. Aadil and Gurudas looked at each other, smiling sheepishly. They had often read about the love stories of Reshma and Vakil Saab in the newspapers.

Vakil Saab got very excited when he read the invitation card. He got a suit stitched specially for the occasion. As he left for the programme that evening, with a song in his heart and a smile on his face, he looked like a king riding on a horse to meet his princess. Vakil Saab's car reached the hotel with police cars following him for protection. Since the time somebody had tried to shoot Vakil Saab, he always had police protection in public functions as he had become a famous man.

Reshma was waiting at the hotel entrance to receive Vakil Saab. Looking beautiful in a black evening gown. Her fair skin, shining like a Kohinoor diamond. She was very slim and petite, while Vakil Saab was on the heavier side. Aadil would jokingly tell Gurudas sometimes that "Vakil Saabs neck must be the same size as Reshma's waist."

Vakil Saab greeted Reshma with a bouquet of flowers. Reshma accepted the bouquet with a big smile on her lips and kissed Vakil Saab's cheeks with a lot of love and excitement. He bent down and started humming a song in her ears to shower her with love. This prompted the media to start clicking pictures and there was a torrent of flashlights clicking away.

Reshma took Vakil Saab to the stage, holding his hand unabashedly, as the whole world knew about their relationship and knew that Vakil Saab loved her a lot. Music Director Vindu and CEO of the HMC company Ramesh Bhatnagar were on the stage along with the Lyricist Bhagat Veer Chandra. There was an announcement and a small little saree-clad girl came and gave everybody the CD. Everyone opened the CD cover and the Music CD was launched amongst a thunderous applause. The room was echoing with claps and Reshma's songs. Everybody was ecstatic with the launch and the songs seemed to be superhit.

At the same party was a very unhappy man by the name of Sham Duggal, sitting in a corner, looking very morose. He was a producer whose film was rotting in the cans and had overshot the budget. He did not know how to handle it, as some small-time goons including Rupesh Kumar were troubling him and not letting him complete the shoot. They would demand all sorts of things which would stall the shoot. When he saw Vakil Saab he thought of including him in the project, so that the goons would stop troubling him. Shyam Duggal went up to Aadil and asked for financial help and said that if Vakil Saab's name is associated with the film it would be profitable to both of them. Aadil too found this offer quite interesting.

Aadil mentioned about the offer to Vakil Saab. When he heard about the offer he immediately agreed but on one condition; Reshma would sing all the songs for the movie. Shyam Duggal had no problem with it. This is how Vakil Saab's Bollywood journey began.

Vakil Saab needed a way to make his illegal earnings legal. His assistant Gurudas was a commerce graduate and he was very attracted to Bollywood and so Gurudas was put at the helm of the Bollywood venture. The music rights, the satellite rights and many such things were well handled by Gurudas. He turned out to be an expert in the filmy world. Which film will do well and which film will need more finance was an easy game for him. This knack made him popular in the filmy world and he was showered with wealth and fame.

As their film association grew, films financed by Vakil Saab would have Reshma as their singer. Reshma's life changed drastically, from poverty to a lavish lifestyle. Though Reshma was famous, her heart did not change. She loved Vakil Saab with the same intensity. Sometimes she would sing jokingly that "Vakil Saab is totally mine, though we are not married."

Not only was she a faithful woman, she was also a great artiste who worshipped Devi Sharda though she was a muslim. She respected every religion as much as her own. Sometimes she would bow down in front of the Cross in a Church, close her eyes and pray.

Mumbai, a huge world in its own right, was now ruled by Vakil Saab. He considered himself as a God of that world. For Muslims he was a Messiah and for Hindus he was an incarnation of the Lord. Vakil Saab held both the communities in equal respect.

Gurudas' commerce degree gave him an edge in the film business and he started earning very well. When Vakil Saab saw his sincerity towards films he started a Production House called "Gurudas Films Private Limited." In the early days people with issues and problems joined this production. However after some time people who wanted to make really good films started to work with them too. Popular and famous heroes and heroines started working in their films. Gurudas Films had made a big name now and about five hundred people were working under this banner. Gurudas looked after everybody in his company as his own family.

Vakil Saab was blessed with a sharp mind and he started making money without any effort now. His main businesses were land, construction and films, giving him a strong hold over Mumbai. He distributed his business between Aadil and Gurudas.

Intelligent and peace loving people did not have any problems with Vakil Saab but a few people like Bhau despised his reign over Mumbai. It is often said that a panther does not lose his stripes. The same way Bhau could not change his nature.

In those days, the two communities, i.e. the Hindus and Muslims were living together with a lot of love and peace. There was no enmity between these two communities. However, as time passed, there were bomb blasts and terrorist encounters. People walking on the streets were never sure whether they would reach home safely.

(In recent times the situation is different and it is thanks to the new Government.)

On one such occasion the sanctity of our Parliament Building was tarnished by some traitors and it really shook the foundation of the Indian Government. Haider Ansari was one of those traitors who was arrested and put behind bars. He was enjoying the free food doled out to him in the prison by the government. What he did not know was that suddenly one day he would receive a call from the Lord Almighty, as he was very sure that his supporters outside the prison would save his neck from the noose. All his calculations failed when he was put to death by hanging, without any court proceedings and without informing the media, as the situation was very dangerous. Haider created a big scene before he was executed but the Government lawyer Budhaji Parab did not let him have his way and he was hung by the neck till he died.

Now they had a very sensitive situation at hand. Haider's relatives were pressuring the Government to bury him in the Mahim dargah. This idea was rejected by the people who loved their country. They said they did not want a traitor buried on their land.

This situation was like a volcano waiting to erupt. The body was ready to be buried in a land laden with gunpowder, waiting for a big explosion. Mahim area was cordoned off by laying Section 144 under the Indian constitution. The joint Commissioner had an urgent meeting with the Crime Branch to sort the situation.

Everybody agreed on one point, that Ansari's body should be taken out in an ambulance with Rampal in the front seat, so that he could control the situation, as he knew the police and the goons equally well. The situation did simmer down a little bit because of Rampal's presence. He was out of jail for just one day but that helped Vakil Saab's gang a lot. He delivered an important message which created ripples in the otherwise peaceful Vakil gang. Rampal informed them that their lives were in danger and a threat was looming over their heads.

Aadil was not worried about his own life but he increased Vakil Saab's security. He wondered if his arch enemy Bhau was already defeated than who would be interested in killing Vakil Saab. Just when Aadil was having these thoughts, his mobile rang and the screen flashed his father's name. His father's name was Husain Khan and mother's name was Farzana. The moment he picked up the phone to answer, he heard loud noises in the background.

His father seemed distressed, he said "Aadil you come home fast."

Aadil: What is it Abbu and why all the noise?"

Hussain: "You just come home."

Aadil: "I will be there soon but tell me one thing. Is everything okay?" Hussain gave the mobile to Farzana asking Aadil to talk to his mother.

Aadil: "Why don't you tell me what the matter is?"

Farzana: "Aadil please come home fast"

Aadil asked her too what the problem was.

Farzana: "Your Aunt, Fauzia Aapa is here."

Aadil: "So what?"

Farzana: "So you come home fast then we will tell you what the matter is'"

Aadil was losing his temper slowly and it seeped in his voice too. He raised his voice a little bit.

Aadil: "Why don't you tell me what is wrong?"

Farzana: "Fauzia Aapa has come with Nasreen. Here, you talk with her."

Aadil lost his temper now.

Aadil: "I don't want to talk with anyone. Nobody is making any sense. I'll be home in sometime."

Saying this, he cut the call and left for home.

When Aadil reached home, everyone was waiting with a sad face. Nasreen was sitting in a corner looking guilty. She looked like she had been crying. When Aadil realized that nobody was saying anything he asked his father what the matter was. Hussain dilly dallied awkwardly and looked at Farzana and said "You tell him...," Farzana said, Arre this Nasreen is..." and she looked over to Fauzia Aapa and said "Aapa you tell him, I can't say anything." Aapa looked at Hussain and requested him to tell Aadil everything. Aadil lost his temper very badly and shouted "Will somebody say something?" Aapa looked at Nasreen and started to say something about how she was cheated. Just then Hussain said "I will tell you my son. It Is about Nasreen..." Suddenly Farzana interrupted him and started talking too.

Aadil pulled his hair in frustration and shouted "Please for God's sake tell me what exactly has happened." Suddenly Nasreen, who was quiet all this time, shouted "I am the culprit, I have made a mistake, just kill me." Fauzia got very angry. She said "Just shut up or else I will really kill you. You have made a complete mess" and turning towards Farzana she said "Farzana you finished getting Aadil and Nasreen married so that we can relax and not worry about Nasreen."

As it is, Aadil was worried about Vakil Saab's security and the moment Aadil heard the word marriage, he was infuriated. He shouted "What has she done that all of you are thinking about marrying her off." Farzana erupted like a volcano now and her real problems poured out. She said "This stupid girl wanted to join a beauty parlour class so I paid the fees. The shameless girl lied to me and was going to acting classes. She wants to be seen on TV and wants to become a Heroine." Now Aadil knew what the problem was and he felt a sense of relief. He asked "Is this the only reason or it is something else. If Nasreen wants to learn acting then let her do it. What is wrong with that? After she finishes the course I will help her get work in our production. Everybody has a right to dream. No one should stop anybody from doing what they want. Please for God's sake don't trouble her."

Hussain did not like what he was hearing. He said "Look what he is saying. If elders are showing them the correct way they don't like it. They consider us as tyrants. You will have to listen to what I am saying. I don't like that a girl from our family would put on makeup and work in front of the camera. "Aadil continued, he said "You are right. We don't like what our elders say because they don't understand our feelings. Fauzia Aapa and Farzana both had understood by now that it is futile to talk with Aadil. Nasreen was very happy and it showed on her face as Aadil was on her side.

Aadil got up and said "Nasreen will continue her acting course. Nobody will say anything or stop her, Khuda Hafiz." He started going down the stairs and Nasreen followed him. Nasreen called out to him and Aadil stopped. With a lot of gratitude she said "Thank you Aadil for helping me. You have always helped me since we were children. You have always supported me." Aadil just smiled and ran down the stairs. Nasreen kept looking at his receding back with a lot of love and longing. Her mind took her down the memory lane and she remembered how they were friends when they were children too.

Aadil and Nasreen had grown up together and Nasreen shared everything with Aadil since the time they were kids. She would even share her food with him as both of them liked the same type of food.

Her mother would always tell her "Nasreen when you grow up you will be married to Aadil. He will be your husband. 'Aadil's mother too agreed with this idea. When both of them turned teenagers they would go to see films together. There was not much left to be said between the two of them.

Aadil was a daredevil by nature and he did things differently. Nasreen felt protected by Aadil and felt a sense of security in his arms. When she was young she would mimic Madhuri Dixit very well, a well known Bollywood star in those years. Her dream was to become a big star and shine in the Bollywood skies as she knew she was immensely beautiful. This was in the good old days when both of them were young.

Coming back to the present day, it was a Sunday morning and Vakil Saab received a message that Aamir Lala wanted to meet him. They were very old friends. Vakil Saab worked on a path of principles and Aamir

Lala also worked just like him. Aamir Lala had a grand history. He had a valiant heart and he spent his whole life believing strongly in his principles.

He started his life working at the docks, smuggling goods, but soon he created a big empire. Many boys from Dongri worked under him. Vakil Saab and Aamir Lala were a great source of support for each other. He lived in a terrace flat on Lamington Road for many years. He also owned a Farm House in Panvel. Whenever he went to Panvel, a bunch of trained acrobatic pigeons also accompanied him. He had a penchant for pigeons and he had a variety of species of pigeons as pets. He would make them perform many acrobatic stunts. When he would reach Panvel he would open their cages and let them fly free in the open skies and they would reach the Lamington Road terrace flat the next day without fail.

Recently Lala was turning deaf in both the ears at the old age of eighty and had to wear hearing aids in both ears. He did not have many relatives alive, friends too had met their creator. He had a very handsome nephew, Samir, who died at the young age of twenty four. It was believed that he was murdered by Aamir Lala himself but the case was closed as there was no evidence. The world of crime did not need evidence. At the same time nobody dared say anything against Amir Lala.

Aamir Lala was a teetotaller, he never gambled, and he never visited prostitutes. He did not have any vices which were common with the crime world. He held his principles in high order and for him there was nothing above it. The people who were dealing with him were too scared of him to deal in drugs like Charas, Ganja and Afeem. He hated drugs and the addiction which came with it. Aamir Lala soon realized that Samir was dealing with drug dealers and doing business with them. He used the fear of Lala they had in their hearts as a means to do his business. When Aamir tried to talk Samir out of it, it was too late. Samir had already tasted the excitement which comes with money. He did not listen and retorted back "Oh come on Uncle, these are different times. Stop talking about old times. If you don't match your steps with the new generation they will walk all over you." When Aamir heard Samir talk in this manner, his blood boiled. He said "Who will walk over me? This new generation that you are talking about? After all those drugs they will not have the strength to do anything. Arre this addiction will reduce their child producing capability. Forget about this business and promise me that you will never deal in drugs." This irritated Samir and he said "Uncle you just do your prayers regularly and don't bother about me." Saying this he just left, banging the door on his way out. Aamir Lala was stunned. He realized that Samir was not under his control anymore.

The smugglers syndicate started questioning him too. They said "Lalaji, you do not allow us to do any drug business but you allow your nephew to do it. This is not fair. We too like to earn more money." He was very hurt by their statement. His own blood had stabbed him in the back. He said "I don't deserve this position now." But everybody from the syndicate disagreed with him. They said "No Lalaji, you truly deserve the chair. You can't leave." That day Lala sat through the meeting with his head bent down and Samir was murdered after a few days.

Times had changed drastically and people did not have scruples anymore. They could betray their country within a split second. There was a battle raging between the traitors and the patriots. There was blood shed on the road. People who loved the Peaceful Mumbai said "Somebody has cast an evil eye on our Mumbai"

Aadil was driving Vakil Saab's Rolls Royce, the policemen were in Vakil Saab's Ambassador car, following them. Both the cars reached Aamir Lala's house on Lamington Road. Aadil had informed Aamir Lala's manager of their trip earlier in the day. Aamir Lala's apartment door was huge and wide, like an emperor's palace gate. The Constable given by the police force for protection entered the apartment and checked whether everything was in order and let them inside. Aamir Lala was sitting in his very large living room wearing a white Pathani suit, and he had on Peshawari Shoes with Zari work on his feet. He also had a beautiful Iranian silk scarf on his shoulder. His weary eyes could not bear the bright light anymore, so he wore dark glasses now. When he saw Vakil Saab he got up from his chair without any support and hugged him with a lot of love. Aadil also bowed down to pay his respects. Aamir's face was shining in spite of his age. Aamir's Khansama (chef) came from the kitchen with glasses of Sharbat (cold drink) and bowed down to Vakil Saab. Lala told the chef "Shamshuddin, Purshottam has come today."

Shamshuddin smiled and replied "Respected Sir, the kebabs are ready to be fried and served." Aamir Lala was a very old friend so he called Vakil Saab by his name. Even the old Chef knew what to cook for Vakil Saab as he knew his favorite cuisine.

Lala said "Then bring it fast. Our stomachs are grumbling. We are ravenous." Everybody started laughing and the atmosphere became lighter. Vakil Saab always had Kebabs when he came here. After Shamshuddin went to the kitchen, Vakil Saab asked Lala "So Lala, why did you call me. "Lala adjusted his hearing Machine in his ears and said "You must have got the news. Your life is in danger. "Vakil Saab replied "Yes we did get the news." Aamir Lala said "So this news is confirmed. The drug mafia wants you out of their way." Aadil asked Lalaji whether he knew who the enemy was.

Lala's face was red with anger. He shouted "You have thousands of enemies. You just have to finish one and the others will kneel down in respect. I know that you too want the same things as me and don't want to be involved in any drug deals. I am aware of your principles, so I want you to stay safe and alive. You need to safeguard the new generation and teach them the right ideals."

Aadil said "I think Bhau is the enemy." Lala retorted that Bhau was not capable of hurting Vakil Saab by himself. He added "Look out, find out who is helping Bhau and make his life miserable." As he finished his sentence he looked at his Secretary. As their eyes met, the Secretary nodded in agreement and went to the other room. When he came out he was carrying a small box in his hand which he placed in front of Aamir Lala. He opened the box, took out an eighties pistol and put it in Vakil Saab's hand and said "Purshottam I am growing old. Allah may call me anytime. I had saved this Pistol for you." When Aamir Lala was giving the pistol to Vakil Saab it seemed as if Lord Krishna was telling Arjuna to get up and fight. He was telling him "Get up Arjuna. Destroy your enemies." The sound of the conch shell, announcing the beginning of the battle, filled the room. It was a very pious moment. Vakil Saab picked up the Pistol, kissed it and bent his head in respect. That evening Vakil Saab enjoyed Shamshuddin's kebabs with a happy heart.

The common man is always crazy about film stars and the film stars were crazy about Vakil Saab. The popularity of stars working with Gurudas film production was reaching the skies. Vakil Saab's name was included in the list of the rich and famous people of Mumbai, whose Rolls Royce's were flying on the roads of Bombay. Vakil Saab's dream of owning a Rolls Royce was now fulfilled.

Reshma Billi was now a popular singer in Bollywood and she considered Vakil Saab her husband. Though no name could be given to their relationship, it was better in so many ways than a husband-wife's. If one would view things with a different perspective, one would see that everybody in Vakil Saab's gang was a good human being. Aadil was ready to sacrifice his life for Vakil Saab. He respected Vakil Saab as much as his Father. Whenever he paid his respects at Pedro Baba's Dargah, he would pray for Vakil Saab's long life. He knew the list of Vakil Saab's enemies was growing longer, as the Bombay mafia gang wanted to deal in drugs without any fear.

Gurudas too would do anything for Vakil Saab. Every Tuesday while going to Siddhivinayak Temple he prayed for Vakil Saab too. Reshma was no less. Although she was on a higher pedestal of popularity she had not forgotten how Vakil Saab had helped her reach there. When she entered this big city called Bombay, she just had a little cash and a bag full of courage with her. But today she had everything. The reason for this was Vakil Saab. People were scared of him.

Vakil Saab had one more humble and pure person in his gang, called Rampal. His hard work was never appreciated in Bhau's gang nor was he ever promoted.

He was always considered a small-time con man. His conscience and values were murdered every day. He was tied down with chains of slavery. He was tired of the dishonour done to him. But one day he took a leap of faith and he was embraced by the love and honour of the Vakil gang. He was just a few days away from freedom.

The Vakil gang was truly Vakil Saab's family. Whenever they got a chance, they would get together, sit on the floor and share their lunch or dinner on a big dastarkhan (tablecloth). Vakil Saab had a habit of eating with his fingers, not a spoon and he loved a dish called Khichada made by his mother, cooked with a lot of whole Spices and a lot of Ghee (clarified butter) in it. The ghee in it made the dish very tasty. Vakil Saab believed that food should be so tasty that people should lick their fingers.

As time went by, his fathers death anniversary came closer. The community priest suggested doing a puja in Modadham, a town near Siddhpur, Gujarat, to help the departed soul reach the gates of heaven. Vakil Saab started preparations for the trip. Aadil booked his flight tickets too. Since the time Rampal had informed them of a threat to Vakil Saab's life, Aadil stayed very close to him. They left for Siddhpur the day prior to the anniversary. It was a three hour drive from Ahmedabad airport and Vakil Saab's security was of utmost importance. Aadil had asked the Gujarat police for protection and they had provided them with two police constables. As an added precaution Aadil had also got two bodyguards from Bombay. There were two jeeps in the front and the back of Vakil Saab's car. The police constables were in the first jeep and the bodyguards were in the jeep at the back. The whole caravan started moving and Vakil Saab reached Sidhpur with his mother without any untoward incident. The priests had already made all the puja preparations. Vakil Saab wore a white new dhoti and sat down for the puja. The atmosphere was filled with the sounds of chants and shlokas recited by the priests.

Food was being prepared for the hundred and one priests who had come for the puja. Aadil had covered his head with a cloth out of respect and was keeping a strict eye on the big gathering as he was worried about Vakil Saab's security. He suddenly noticed that a priest was trying to go near Vakil Saab over and over and he appeared to be stressed. His eyes were constantly flitting all over the area. His feet did not feel in tandem with his brain. He was constantly touching his waist as if he had hidden something there. Aadil's eyes were following him everywhere. When the priest realized that Aadil was observing him, he just stopped in his tracks. Now Aadil was certain that something was off with the priest. Aadil got up and started moving towards him, piercing his way through the crowd.

Aadil looked down to his waist to check his revolver and immediately looked up again but the priest took advantage of that moment and he vanished. Aadil rushed to Vakil Saab's side and he alerted the bodyguard too, but that priest could not be found. By the time the puja was complete, it was nearing evening time. The priest lit a diya (lamp) on a peepal leaf and asked Vakil Saab to release it into the river Godavari. It is believed that if a dead man's wishes have not been completed the diya returns to the bank of the river. The diya did not return and Vakil Saab and his mother were relieved that his wishes were already fulfilled and they felt as if he had broken all his ties and his soul was happy to be in Modadham. The priest said "The floating diya indicates that your father and your ancestors are happy with the puja and now the future will be very auspicious and happy."

The moment the puja was over Aadil took Vakil Saab and his mother to a secret place. He called for a sketch artist and gave him minute details about the man who had vanished. As Aadil started describing him, the talented artist started making a sketch. When the sketch was complete Aadil immediately said "This is the man I had seen. He was standing right here." He called a meeting with his security team and showed them the sketch so that they could start looking out for him without wasting another second.

The next day Vakil Saab and his mother left Siddhpur for Ambaji. It was a two hour drive. When they reached Ambaji his mother recounted how he had the mundan ceremony (tonsure ceremony) in Ambaji when he was younger. Ambaji was their ancestral deity (Kuldevi). Judge Saab too believed in the deity and had immense reverence for Her. He would visit the temple at least twice in a year. There are fifty one established Shakti Peeth and reverants who come here to bow their heads.

As they neared the temple Vakil Saab moved ahead to pay his respects. The accompanying Brahmin priest had informed them about a small puja, so Vakil Saab sat down with his mother to perform the puja. They were surrounded by security on Aadil's orders. The bodyguardsfrom Mumbai too had taken their positions. The puja lasted for two hours. Aadil was watching everything like a hawk.

Now it was time to pay respects to the temple of Ambe Maa, the Goddess at Gabbar, which was located on a small hill. Vakil Saab sat in the helicopter with his mother and after reaching the top they sprinkled flowers on the temple and prayed for the well being of their family. Aadil was still alert and was scanning the area diligently. He was worried about just one thing, and that was Vakil Saab's security. Aadil was still looking out for the man who went missing at Siddhpur and his face was ingrained in his memory.

Now only one town near Ambaji, called Kumbhariya, was in their list and all of them reached Kumbhariya. Vakil Saab and his mother bowed their heads to the deity. Their religious journey was now complete without any interruption. They stayed back that night. They were supposed to leave early next morning for Ahmedabad. The private bodyguards and the police took care of Vakil Saab's security for the night but Aadil could not sleep. The information given by Rampal could not be wrong. The face of the priest was imprinted in his mind. He lay wide awake all night thinking about all this.

The next morning, the caravan of cars left Ambaji in the early hours. The cars were speeding on the road. The cool morning breeze was making Vakil Saab sleepy and he put his head on the seat to sleep. Suddenly the first car signalled to stop. All the cars stopped one by one. Aadil got out of the car in a swift moment and asked the driver "What is wrong?" The driver said, "Sir, the car tyre is punctured." Before they knew it the tyres of all the other cars were also punctured.

Aadil was wondering why all the car tyres were punctured at the same place. But luckily there was a stepney in all the cars. He went back a few steps and he saw nails lying on the road. He looked around but it was early in the morning and it was still dark. He was thinking that this could be a plot against Vakil Saab. Just then the silence was broken with the reverberating sound of bullets. The bullets were coming from the nearby bushes. The policemen took their positions immediately and started shooting towards the bushes. Aadil immediately lay on the ground trying to escape the bullets. Nobody was visible but the bullets had not stopped. Aadil immediately understood that the nails on the road were a plot to stop the cars there. The bodyguards had already stationed themselves around Vakil Saab's car. Aadil wanted to go near Vakil Saab but the bullets were coming from both the sides. Suddenly he heard a scream from the bushes. Aadil understood that somebody was hurt as the firing suddenly stopped. Police started slowly crawling towards the place from where the screams were coming. There was an injured man lying in the bushes. He was shot in the knee. He was trying to control his whimpering but he was in too much pain. The revolver lying next to him was empty. The police started beating him mercilessly. He started bleeding from his mouth and he was shrieking in pain. Aadil put on his mobile light to look at his face and he was taken aback. He was the same priest who was trying to go near Vakil Saab in Siddhpur and the same man whose sketch was made by the police artist. He was planning to kill Vakil Saab in Siddhpur, but because of Aadil's strict security he could not do that. So he made another plan. But it proved to be unlucky too.

The police asked the man "Who is your partner in this game?" He was in great pain. He answered in a quivering voice "Rawa Singh, Rawa singh is my partner." The police were shocked. They asked him, "Are you Jora Singh." He immediately agreed. The whole area was terrified of the two dacoits. They were famous for robberies and kidnapping in North Gujarat. Every political party took their help during elections. Their criminal activities knew no bounds. After a while the police van arrived from Palanpur and took Jora Singh and admitted him in the Civil Hospital. The Gujarat police escorted Vakil Saab and his companions to Ahmedabad airport in their van.

Within three hours, by that time the sun had come up, the news had spread to the Media. A swarm of journalists were waiting for them at the airport. Everybody was asking just one question "Who planned to kill you and why?" Vakil Saab answered very diplomatically "I just have one answer to all your questions. I did not know anything about this attack and if you are asking me who did it, then the Gujarat police will give you an answer. Although I would surely like to ask the Gujarat Government this, that you put up big hoardings and invite us to Gujarat, do you welcome us with bullets?"

The next day Vakil Saab's statement was printed on the front page of all the Gujarati newspapers. The Gujarat Government took this statement very seriously and asked the Home Minister to initiate an enquiry. Gujarat police wanted to save their prestige. They gathered all the informants and started the search.

They found Rawa singh in a slum near an old British railway station of Dhanwada. He was relaxing in the hut with alcohol in his hand, without a worry in the world. Four policemen in civil dress code entered the hut. The moment they saw him wearing a red turban they guessed that it was Rawa Singh. Rawa Singh was a very crafty impersonator. He could put up a good performance if required and he was a good linguist too. He could speak many languages. He had tied a Rajasthani style turban on his head and had worn a dhoti below to blend with the local Marwadis and fool the police.

Before capturing him, the policemen wanted to be certain of his identity, as they didn't want to cause any further damage to their image. The four policemen sat near Rawa Singh and ordered a lota of the alcohol (They served alcohol not in glasses but in a lota, a pitcher). The moment Rawa Singh noticed unknown people around him, he immediately sensed something was off. He tried to remember whether he knew them from anywhere. He had already finished one pitcher of alcohol and had started another one. The cunning Rawa Singh recognised the four policemen in no time. He was now very sure of their identity. He had previously managed to fool the police many times so he was a little relaxed. At the same time the police had recognised him too. Constable Ramabhai Valan swiftly got up from his seat and aiming a gun at him said in a stern voice, "Rawa Singh the police jeep is just outside. Come on get in." Rawa Singh looked around him and realised that he was surrounded by constables. He did not lose his cool and replied in the Rajasthani language "I think sir you are making a mistake. My name is Kalu Bhati and I am from Dungarpur Rajasthan. "While talking to Ramabhai he picked up the pitcher and finished his drink in a big gulp and added "If you don't believe me I can show you my Identity Card." While saying this he brandished a revolver from a small bundle near his feet and fired at Ramabhai. Ramabhai fell down instantly and the whole hut was splattered with his blood. Rawa Singh ran from the hut with the agility of an animal and the confused people in the hut started running helter skelter out of fear. For a moment the other three policemen could not understand what had happened. Rawa Singh jumped over the barbed wire fence and entered the farm around the hut. One constable took care of Ramabhai and the other two followed Rawa Singh immediately. Ramabhai was taken to the nearby Patan Hospital. There was a lot of bleeding but he was still alive as the bullet had scraped past his heart. Two brave constables Jivabhai Bhai and Dharmabhai Rawal followed Rawa Singh and killed him in the farm. This operation was completed by the Gujarat police in a record forty eight hours and they were highly praised for this feat. The constables who had successfully killed Rawa Singh received many messages congratulating them. Many institutes gave them cash prizes too, as people were happy to get rid of a dangerous dacoit like him. At the same time the police were successful in digging out the truth from Jora singh in the Hospital. The police delved deep and dug out the truth.

Vakil Saab's life was worth fifty lakh only. The contract to kill him was given to Rawa Singh by a Secretariat peon called Sadanand. He was paid an advance of twenty five lakhs and the remaining amount was to be paid after the job was completed. The fact that a Secretariat peon had paid this huge sum was very surprising. Tracking the chain connecting the peon to the original culprit was easy. After receiving the Gujarat police's statement, it was Mumbai police's turn to take things forward. The peon Sadanand was traced to his hut in Vikhroli which was found locked. He hailed from Nasik so the police went to Nasik but they realised that he had never gone to Nasik. It was over two days that they were trying to find him, but they could not trace Sadanand.

Vakil Saab was sitting with Aadil in a room which could be called a torture room. The walls were dark and eerie, and the light from a single bulb fell on a half dead man lying on the floor. He could not bear the glare of the light falling on his face. He had already spewed everything he knew to Vakil Saab and Aadil in these three days. The man lying here was the same Sadanand that the police had been searching for. Aadil had managed to kidnap him after receiving the police information. Sadanand was just a pawn in this game dancing to the tunes of others like a puppet.

A newly elected politician had started making statements against the Government. He misled his community and had managed to make a successful political career out of it. A few years ago he used to work in a little flour mill but now he was moving around in a lavish car, thanks to the cash he swindled from trusting people. He was Shevantilal. He had a knack of making people do his dirty work for him. He had the gift of the gab, a sweet talker and he knew exactly how to play with people's emotions.

This was the same man who had paid Sadanand twenty lakhs. The moment Aadil heard Shevantilal's name, he dug out all the details of his life. Shevantilal was a very good friend of Bhau's son Rupesh kumar. Now slowly but surely the links were opening up. Aadil was not in a big hurry to grapple with him. He wanted to wait and watch. Shevantilal had attacked like a sly vulture, but Vakil Saab was unharmed.

Aadil strategically avoided doing anything for a few months, to tire the enemy. This way he could guess the enemy's strategy before anybody could.

Today was Thursday and Aadil as usual had returned from Pedroshah's dargah after paying his respects. Nasreen too entered right behind him with a packet of sweets and she put a sweet in Aadil's mouth. Aadil asked "Why did you bring sweets Nasreen? What is the occasion?." Nasreen excitedly showed him the certificate "Look, I stood first in my acting class. Today Subhash Ghai, the well known Director watched my drama and he was praising my work. Now will I get to work in a film?" Aadil just kept looking at Nasreen. She looked like a fresh fragrant flower. Today the whole world looked like a garden. When she was a kid she used to save her pocket money. After saving a big amount she would hold Aadil's hand and take him to the sweet shop. She would say "Come Aadil, I have some cash with me. We will eat Barfi." She still had the same innocence she had when they were younger. Aadil felt as if both of them were innocent kids again.

Aadil pulled her leg as usual. He said "Suppose I say no then what will you do?" Nasreen got irritated as usual but within a second she was like a child. Aadil added "I can say no. I can say that I won't give you work in films. I could say that I cannot go against my parents." Aadil could read many questions in the lines forming on Nasreen's forehead. She stood quietly for some time and said "You had said that day in front of everyone that you would give me work in your production." Aadil said "Yes I did say that, but I can always change my mind." Nasreen's beautiful flower-like face began wilting. She seemed disappointed and tears welled up in her eyes. Aadil realized that and instantly stopped teasing her. He picked up his phone in an instant and called Gurpal and informed him about Nasreen completing her acting course. He told him that Nasreen had come with a box of sweets as she had aced the acting course and Subhash Ghai had praised her acting immensely.

Though they had already made preparations for Nasreen's debut, Aadil asked her to talk to Gurudas. He said "You start coming to the office from tomorrow. A script is ready for you. You will be doing the lead role and Vakil Saab will launch you." When she heard everything, she started jumping in delight. She felt as if she had wings and she was flying in the big blue sky and the light white clouds were flying with her too. She was on cloud nine.

Vakil Saab had moved ahead in life. His life had always been full of crime and controversies but he had good people working under him. He had a tendency of picking up good habits from people he respected. He had faced a lot of upheavals in his life but he had always remained calm. He always felt his father's blessings protecting him from all the mishaps in his life.

And as his age was progressing he was losing interest in his business and was veering towards sainthood and spirituality. He had reduced his alcohol intake too. Sometimes he would wear saffron coloured clothes like a sadhu and sit in his office or meditate. This gave him immense peace. He also wore a string of Rudraksha around his neck and a mala worn like a bracelet around his wrist, which the Mahatma had given him. He was very much attracted to Kailash Mansarovar, a beautiful location in the Himalayas known for its religious and spiritual importance. He always sat with his eyes closed thinking about Kailash. When he meditated he always felt the cool breeze from the snow capped mountains around him.

One day while he was enjoying the peace and the quiet around him, he suddenly heard the chanting of Shiv Tandava stotram (a Sanskrit hymn recited to sing praises of Lord Shiva). And with that stotra ringing in his ears, Aadil entered Vakil Saab's office and announced that somebody wanted to meet him.

When that man entered his office, Vakil Saab noticed his south Indian attire. He looked very worried and disturbed. It was obvious he needed Vakil Saab's help. Aadil asked him, "What do you want?" He immediately replied in broken Hindi with a thick South Indian accent, "Humko... ek....supari dena mangta…" Vakil Saab looked at him so the man said "Hum Kerala se hai. Humko Hindi nahi aata. English aata." "Do we look like contract killers?" Aadil asked. "Aiyo no Sir. I don't want to kill him, I just want to scare him so that he leaves Bombay." Vakil Saab lit a cigarette, put it to his lips in his inimitable style and said "Don't say Bombay say Mumbai." "Yes yes yes... Mumbai. He will leave Mumbai and go to the village." Aadil asked "Why do you want him to leave Mumbai?" The South Indian replied with a worried look, "If he does not leave he will commit suicide Sir." Vakil Saab could gauge this man instantly. He could sense that he was genuinely worried about something. He did not know how to handle the situation. Aadil asked him who this person was. But instead of that man Vakil Saab replied. "He is his son." The moment that man heard this he sat down near Vakil Saab's feet. He could not believe his ears. "You are like a God Sir '' he said. He wondered how Vakil Saab understood his misery so instantly. Vakil Saab immediately got up and embraced him. This gesture touched his heart and he broke down into tears, all his worries flowing out with them. Vakil Saab ordered Aadil to get some tea for that man. Sipping the hot cup of tea relaxed him and he started narrating his story "Aiyo sir, you see I have a hundred coconut trees and hundred betel nut trees in the village. We are well to do and we do not have any debts on our head. My son Ramanuj loved acting since school time. He watched a lot of Hindi movies. He would copy them so well that he started speaking Hindi very fluently, but sorry sir I can't speak Hindi well. He did an acting course after he finished college. Then he came to Bombay… sorry Mumbai. He had to struggle but he got a role in a television serial after some time. The serial was popular so he got an offer for a film after that. The film was a big hit. He made a big name in the village too. People chanted Ramanuj Ramanuj Ramanuj! in our village. He then went on to sign four more films under a big banner. And now… one by one he was thrown out of all the four films. He called me and cried a lot. There is a lot of politics in this industry. He is mentally broken with all the politics and now he is in depression. I tried to pacify him and asked him to come back to the village with me but he refuses to budge from here. That is why I came to you. Please help me!"

Aadil said "Vakil Saab, Ramanuj is a very good actor."

"Which production house does he work for?" asked Vakil Saab. The man immediately replied "Verma Production."

Aadil immediately made a call to Raj Verma of Verma Production. Raj Verma picked up the phone. Aadil told him that Vakil Saab wanted to talk to him and handed him the phone. As soon as he heard Vakil Saab's name, Raj sprung up from his Chair and said "Pranam Vakil Saab, how can I help you Sir." Vakil Saab said "You must be knowing Ramanujan?" Raj Verma immediately understood what was going on and he started giving excuses "Vakil Saab, I could not help it. I did what Bhai told me to do. My production was funded by him. Vakil Saab asked "Who is this Bhai?" Raj answered "He is from Dubai, Bhai Zakir Poison." Vakil Saab banged the phone down and looked at Aadil and asked "Zakir Poison does funding for films too?" Aadil replied "Yes Vakil Saab he has invested a lot of money in films recently." Vakil Saab looked at that man and said "Send Ramanujan to Gurudas Production's office. If your son really has the talent we will launch him in our film. It is a promise. That man again prostrated in front of Vakil Saab's feet and said "I will always be under your obligation." and he started walking towards the door. Aadil asked "What is your name?" He turned around and said "Gopalan", and he left the room in a hurry.

After a couple of days it was Nasreen's film's 'Muhurat day'. It was a Thursday. Nasreen reached the studio with

Aadil. They were the first ones to arrive at the studio. Though she was the Heroine of the film she worked on the set like any other regular Production person. She was always full of enthusiasm. The make-up man came to Nasreen and said "Come Madam, please get your make-up done." Nasreen got up and went to the Green Room (makeup room).

The Director had set up the shot and the lights were also ready. Aadil looked at his watch as he was waiting for Vakil Saab. Nasreen came out of the makeup room. As Aadil turned and looked at Nasreen, he was dumbstruck. She had completely transformed with the makeup and costume. She looked beautiful. Her face shone like a hundred moons shining together. He had never seen Nasreen like this before. Nasreen noticed that Aadil was looking at her without batting his eyelids. Nasreen slowly went near him and whispered "where are you lost Aadil? How do I look?" Aadil was at a loss of words. He simply kept looking at her and Nasreen too was looking into his eyes. Both of them looked ethereal in that moment. Their friendship was so pure that they were ready to sacrifice everything for each other. Aadil prayed for her in his heart and kissed Nasreen's forehead and said "May all the bad omens stay away from you." Nasreen could not believe that she had finally arrived at the destination she had always dreamed of. She was also a little nervous and was sweating underneath her costly costume. The spot boy was standing near her with an umbrella to protect her from the sun. Nasreen was trying to convince herself that she really was the Heroine of the film. The Assistant Director came to her and asked "Madam do you know the dialogues by heart? Let's do a rehearsal." A few moments after Nasreen left with him to rehearse, Vakil Saab entered the set with Reshma on his arm. Vakil Saab had arrived to inaugurate the muhurat shot. When Nasreen heard that Vakil Saab had arrived she ran to him like a little child and touched his feet. Reshma had given playback for Nasreen in this film. All the songs in this film were recorded in Reshma's silky smooth and sweet voice. They were now ready to start shooting. Everybody prayed along with Gurudas singing the Ganesh Vandana and Vakil Saab gave the clap. The Director said "Action" and the shoot started. Nasreen started filming for her first shot. Everybody went silent just listening to her dialogue delivery. When the shot was over, the set was echoing with the sound of claps. Nasreen had really done a good job. In this moment of excitement Aadil suddenly noticed that Nasreen and Gurudas had come closer and he seemed to like the idea.

Gurudas was more than a brother for Aadil and he thought that Gurudas would be a perfect partner for a girl like Nasreen. He wanted Nasreen to always be happy.

In the meanwhile, a man wearing a topi (A hat) managed to reach Vakil Saab after jostling through the crowd with great difficulty. Before the bodyguards and Aadil could react, he went straight to Vakil Saab and fell down at his feet. The bodyguards rushed to Vakil Saab, but Vakil Saab had already bent down and picked him up. When their eyes met, Vakil Saab could not control his emotions and hugged him tightly. Aadil and Gurudas were already at Vakil Saab's side. Rampal's sudden arrival had made Vakil Saab ecstatic but questions were cropping up in his mind. There were still three more months of time left for his release from jail, then how had he arrived so early. Aadil and Gurudas were wondering the same thing. Rampal could see the confusion in their eyes. He said "Vakil Saab with your blessings and my good behaviour I was released early. This was thanks to the lessons I have learnt from you." Rampal's arrival had created excitement in the Vakil gang. Aadil decided to complete all the pending jobs, now that Rampal had arrived. The Vakil gang was complete now and had gained new strength with Rampal's arrival. Aadil's daredevilry, Gurudas' business acumen and Rampal's camaraderie with the policemen and Politicians; it was a very good mix needed for success. Rampal also had his own secret network of people who could dig out secrets and strategies of the opposition gang. This was Rampal's strong suit and it strengthened the Vakil gang foundation. He had already gathered a lot of new information while in prison. They got to work right away and planned for tasks which they were going to execute three months later.

They were now seated around the round table in the Conference Room at Vakil Saab's Warehouse. All of them were waiting for Rampal to divulge his information and he started talking. "Bhau has become friends with Shivram, the head of the Porbandar drug mafia, with Shevantilal's help. This new drug called Chilly Poison is entering via the ocean route and is being distributed in Gujarat and Rajasthan by Shivram. He is neck deep in the black money he has earned from the drug deals. He has been behaving like a Prince of some State, since he is hand in glove with the Gujarat police. The glaze of money Bhau is earning in the drug business has blinded him.

He now wants to distribute the Chilly Poison in the whole of Maharashtra but he is scared of you. He wants to regain the name and fame he had lost through this Drug Distribution. The way Shivram was friends with the Gujarat police, Bhau has joined hands with a high-ranking police officer in Maharashtra. If you are eliminated then he will succeed in winning the whole world with his vile ways. In today's times, no other business can make you the amount of profit like the drug business."

When Aadil heard this, he suggested "If Bhau has the police on his side then things can be difficult for us. We should finish off Bhau before he strikes." Vakil Saab was listening intently and gently stroking the Rudraksha beads (holy beads) given to him by the Baba and he said "No son, it will be a precocious decision. We have to find a way whereby he himself comes and embraces death with both his arms. First we have to find out about the police officer who is helping Bhau. Then we will start our game."

Anyway Mumbai was free of the deadly drugs as the underworld was familiar with Vakil Saab's wrath and also his rules and regulations when it came to this topic.

Vakil Saab often said that he is thankful that the enemies across the border were not deceitful and they were open about their shady deals. At least they openly declared that they were our enemies. But in our country we have backstabbers who are like spineless eunuchs, who don't deserve any respect"

Just then Rampal received a message on his mobile. The first drug dispatch had left Porbandar, a town in Gujarat. Shevantilal was supposed to collect the delivery in Mumbai. Bhau had deliberately stayed away from this matter. The Vakil gang moved their first pawn in this game of chess by alerting the Crime Branch Unit. A tempo numbered 'GJ25' arrived in Mumbai after almost 20 hours. Shevantilal confirmed the number, looked around to check if anybody was looking. He went closer to the tempo and asked him in code, "How many stars are there in the sky?" The driver checked Shevantilal's photo on his mobile and told his cleaner(assistant), "Give the box to Saab."

Shevantilal's car was a short distance from the tempo. The Crime Branch officers were waiting nearby in civil dress. The moment Shevantilal took the wares in his hands, the officers surrounded him from all sides. Shevantilal did not lose his cool. When one of the officers asked him about the canister in his hand, he said it contained Ghee (Clarified Butter). There was a label on the canister which read in Gujarati, 'Desi Ghee from Khambhat'. The other officer grabbed the can and opened it immediately. They found drugs inside. Shevantilal very casually said "Sir I had asked for Ghee but if this contains Poison then it is not my fault." The officers arrested the driver and the cleaner and put them in the van. Shevantilal kept arguing but the officer arrested him too. Shevantilal realized that if he is put behind bars he will never be able to come out. He decided that he would do anything to avoid imprisonment. He looked around stealthily, pushed the police man and ran towards the crowded lane nearby. He chose to go that way so that the police could not take a shot at him and his plan succeeded. They could not shoot him and he managed to flee but the police cordoned off the area. Though Shevantilal could not be caught, the police force was happy that they could manage to nab drugs worth twenty crore and the drug mafia network was broken down. The news turned out to be one more nail in Bhau's coffin and the very first drug trade was ruined. Bhau broke all his glass windows in a burst of anger when he heard the news.

When Vakil Saab was asked to comment about the incident, he roared like a lion and said "I am a

Mumbaikar. I will ruin anybody who tries to bring drugs in my Mumbai."

Everyone related to this drug deal had an urgent meeting to discuss how they could recover the twenty crore they had lost. The greedy Shivram tried to put pressure on Bhau. As Bhau was going through a bad time anyway, he immediately washed his hands off and pushed the whole responsibility on Shevantilal. As he was an expert in these games and had proved it by dodging the police successfully.

He started addressing the group in a language all of them could understand. He said "After such a big mess in our racket we cannot put the entire responsibility on one person if we want to save our network. This Vakil Saab has turned us all into crawling insects, but we are not down in the dumps yet. If we want to get out of this, we have to get rid of Vakil Saab. We have to kill him. Are we ready for that?" Shevantilal's words ignited a new fire and everybody's blood started boiling with vengeance. All of them agreed with Shevantilal and signed on Vakil Saab's death warrant. The police officer on whom the whole network depended, also wanted Vakil Saab out of his way. So they could do their vile business without any hassles. The loss of twenty crores had irritated Shivram too. He had never faced such a huge loss. He was constantly saying "If this had happened in Gujarat, I would have got back my goods in no time but this is Mumbai and Vakil

Saab has sent the message straight to the Crime Branch. The drug mafia cannot make any 'under the table' deals with the police."

Shevantilal lit a cigarette, inhaled the smoke with a deep breath and started speaking with great confidence. "I have a lottery worth twenty crores. The twenty crores we lost in a day, I will get back in one night. But we will have to pay one crore for that." Everybody had question marks all over their faces and within a second all of them asked the same question, in the same tone "Twenty crores in one night? But how?" Shevantilal revealed the suspense by telling them "It would be easy if Shivram helped us because everyone here knows that Shivram is very pally with the Gujarat police. Shivram was very excited to just hear about the amount and he immediately said "I'm ready to help you!"

Shevantilal said "The Badshah of the Surat Diamond Industry, Shyam G Sevani, is going to deliver Diamonds polished from the rough diamonds given by an Amsterdam Businessman. Shyam G Sevani's secret mafia has cautioned them that this news has leaked, so they are trying to find different ways of delivering the diamonds safely. The Amsterdam businessman has been pressuring them to deliver the diamonds as soon as possible, so that he can get back to Amsterdam immediately. Shyam G Sevani has stopped trusting his regular courier company. The company now knows that the diamonds that he is planning to send are not worth lakhs but crores. The real price of the rough (unpolished) diamonds was known only to four trusted members. What would the value be after they are polished, how many carats will they weigh, and how will they be sold? Shyam has discussed this with these four trusted members, only behind closed doors.

Shyam is a very righteous and noble person. He is not educated but has built an empire worth millions in Gujarat just by his inner strength. He takes care of thousands of families. He believes that everybody is as noble as him. But in recent times people could sell their own conscience to make more money."

Since Shyam did not trust the courier company, he along with those four trusted members finally appointed a very simple man to be the delivery man for this job. But he was not told that he will be carrying diamonds worth millions to Mumbai. He was told that he is carrying diamonds worth five lakhs to Mumbai. And that somebody would come to receive him at Mumbai station. The man boarded the train from Surat, leaving for Mumbai.

On the other hand Shevantilal had already set up his web to trap Shyam. They planned to kidnap the delivery man, so that the case was given to the Gujarat police, who were friends with Shivram. Until now, Bhau had always considered Shevantilal to be a small goon, but now he was very impressed with his vicious and cunning brain. He thought to himself "I have to save this boy from the law and the police, so that he could become another Rampal, ready to blindly follow anything that he was ordered to do.

Shivram had already called his men from Porbundar and had explained the plan to them. One thing was for sure and made them happy was that they were going to get back the twenty crores they had lost. And it happened exactly as Shivram and Shevantilal had planned. Shyam Sevani's manager was bribed with a few crores and he had revealed the entire plan to Shevantilal. He did something a man with a good soul would never do. As a result, the man who was going to deliver the diamonds was very easily caught in the train, taken away and put to death in cold blood and very cleverly, no proof was left behind.

Shyam Sevani's company and the Gujarat police were running helter skelter, but they could not find anything except the dead body. This news was put on the front page of all the newspapers by a few media people from Gujarat, who were paid to misguide people by spreading fake news. The headlines read that 'The Goons from UP have looted Twenty Crores from Surat in Broad Daylight.' Another newspaper wrote 'The country is in the grips of Jungle Raaj' and they targeted the country's Prime Minister. This newspaper did not like the ruling party from day one and would never let go of a chance to make comments about the Prime Minister. This is why a very famous newspaper had lost its identity once upon a time.

The whole of Gujarat state knew that this newspaper's owner had very good relations with Porbandar's don Shivram. Whenever Shivram's name was mentioned in his media, he was called "The saviour of the poor." He was also called a Bollywood hero, as he spent lakhs on his wardrobe, all of the latest styles and fashion.

Vakil Saab on the other side had started wearing saffron robes, saffron lungis and always had the Rudraksha string around his wrist, which was given to him by the Mahatma. It seemed as if he was giving up the worldly pleasures. Many people wondered about his changing attire. He changed into a black coat when he attended the court but Vakil Saab was a changed man from the inside. His life was really taking a U-turn.

Shivram could not gauge the strength of the Vakil gang. Bhau had convinced Shivram that once Vakil Saab was out of the race, there was nobody in Mumbai who could stop the drug deals from happening. It was the only way they could live without being under the stress of constant terror.

Shivram agreed with what Bhau said and immediately sent two sharpshooters from Porbundar to Mumbai. The Mumbai mafia had already signed on Vakil Saab's death warrant and Shevantilal supplied them with the weapons.

Though Shevantilal was underground he carried on with his drug deals. He was scared of Vakil Saab and Pilas both. He had a feeling that if Vakil Saab was out of his way then his court case would be dismissed and he could be out of this self imposed exile. Shevantilal had already done the recce of Vakil Saab's office, warehouse and Sonali Bar, which he knew he often frequented. He did not know that Vakil Saab had stopped visiting Sonali bar recently.

Vakil Saab always arrived at his office in his Rolls Royce car, at exactly eleven am everyday. Aadil and Vakil Saab were always together in the office. Rampal took care of the warehouse and Gurudas was busy with the film production. Nasreen's film shooting was moving ahead with great speed. In the midst of all this, a romance was blossoming between Gurudas and Nasreen and their names were often mentioned in the newspapers. Vakil Saab had kept Gurudas away from the world of crime. He was earning crores with his sincerity and his accounts were clean too. Gurudas believed that the cleaner your deals are the more profit you make. His common man style of business management is what attracted Nasreen towards Gurudas.

Nasreen was equally simple and straightforward too. She would get up early and cook food to carry to the shoot, though she was the main lead in a film. She never misbehaved on the set. She did her chores sincerely. She would eat the food she brought with Gurudas during the lunch break and discuss the menu for the next day with him. If she had a little free time she would go to the market to buy vegetables too, as people did not recognise her yet. She often travelled by public transport and took the bus or auto rickshaw to reach the shoot location. A girl with such high ideals and very few needs would make any man feel richer than a king. Gurudas felt like a king in her company. He was falling more and more in love with Nasreen. She was an epitome of simplicity. She was tall according to Indian standards and her long neck made her look very graceful. The grace added to her beauty and made her look all the more ethereal. Sometimes nature bestows all the good characteristics in a single person and that person goes on to become the greatest one on the face of the earth, and lives on for a long time in people's memories. Nasreen was one of those. The hard work Nasreen was putting into her film made Gurudas certain that she would become a great star, the moment the film was released. She would surely be remembered for generations to come.

As always Vakil Saab got out of his Rolls Royce, wearing his regular saffron clothes, with his bodyguards in tow. Two sadhus were following them and were in a hurry to get closer to Vakil Saab. The bodyguards barred them from moving forward, so one of the Sadhus told them that they wanted to talk to Vakil Saab. Vakil Saab stopped the moment he heard that and asked them "tell me learned one, what do you want to know." One of the Sadhu said "Can we talk privately?" Vakil Saab asked the bodyguards to wait near the gate. When they reached the gate Vakil Saab looked at the Sadhu and said "Tell me sir, what do you want from me." The sadhu said "Nothing, we will do something for you. Vakil Saab could not understand what he was trying to say so he asked "Something for me?" The second sadhu crossed all limits of civility and said "You did a lot for others but now you do all this after you meet your dear God." While saying this he pulled out a revolver hidden in his Kurta and fired at Vakil Saab. He understood what was happening in a split second. The moment the shot was fired Vakil Saab reacted quickly and ducked. The bullet whizzed past, missing his head. The bodyguards ran towards him and escorted him into a room and locked it and started firing on the sadhus. The moment Aadil heard the sound of the bullet shots he too came running and saw that one of the bodyguards was lying on the floor injured. He immediately took out his gun and started firing. But the hired killers were also skilled at their job. Aadil's six bullets were wasted and nobody was hurt. The moment Aadil realised that his bullets were over he hid himself behind a wall. The killers had only one aim in mind, to kill Vakil Saab. They did not want to waste time pursuing Aadil. They quickly got close to Vakil Saab's room and started shooting on the lock. They were very sure that Aadil's bullets were over. They were firing at the lock without worrying about Aadil so that they could finish their job and get out.

Within a few seconds Aadil took out another revolver he had hidden in his shoe and confronted the killers. He aimed the revolver at the killers and in an unfazed tone said "Now complete the job after you go to hell." He shot at one of the killers. His head burst open like a water filled balloon and his blood splattered all over the walls. Aadil's reckless stance scared the other killer and he was confused. He started running but shot Aadil in the stomach as a last resort. Aadil ignored the pain and kept shooting at the killer. Meanwhile Vakil Saab went through a secret door and came face to face with the shooter. He suddenly stopped when he saw Vakil Saab. Vakil Saab noticed that Aadil was bleeding from the stomach and he was livid. He shot the killer in his leg in retaliation, who started screaming in agony and fell down to the ground. Vakil Saab enjoyed letting him suffer for a while and then shot him in his stomach and asked him "Did you like the taste of this?" The shooter realised that his end had come very close and all his planning was not going to work anymore. In that moment, Vakil Saab looked like Yamraj (the God of Death) to him. And as he watched Death itself, dancing in Vakil Saab's eyes, he could not see the other bullet coming towards him, which brought his end with it.

Aadil was quickly rushed to Kokilaben Hospital in Andheri where a big group of doctors started looking after him. Vakil Saab had taken over Aadil's care and the doctors were also trying their level best to save Aadil. Gurudas and Nasreen immediately reached the hospital, the moment they heard the news. The police had begun their investigation and the shooter's body was sent to Cooper Hospital.

After a lot of struggle the Doctors managed to remove the bullet from Aadil's stomach but the poison had started spreading. By evening, things were getting complicated. His worried parents were crying outside his room. The Doctors had done their best and didn't know what else they could do. They felt helpless and said "He needs blessings now, more than medicines." Vakil Saab sat in a room in his saffron robes and started chanting the Maha Mrutyunjay Jaap.

Om Tryambakam Yajamahe Sugandhim Pushti-Vardhanam

Urvarukamiva Bandhanan Mrityormukshiya Mamritat II

The room resonated with his clear and loud chanting. The media had already gathered outside, waiting for a glimpse of Vakil Saab.

Rampal connected with all his informants to get information on who had ordered this attack as soon as possible.

When Vakil Saab was chanting the mantra, he remembered that it was Thursday; and every Thursday Aadil went to Pedro Baba's Mazar and covered it with flowers. He completed his chant and immediately got up and left without informing anyone. Rampal saw this and followed him with a licensed revolver in his hand. Vakil Saab drove his Rolls Royce himself, with the Bodyguard's Jeep following him.

Both Vakil Saab and Rampal were silent during the ride. The Rolls Royce sped past Crawford Market and reached V.T. Station and stopped in front of Pedro Baba's Mazar. He got out of the car and tied a saffron cloth on his head. By that time the bodyguard had taken their positions. Vakil Saab bought a blanket of flowers, to make an offering at the Tomb. The people around were looking at him, amazed at what they saw. A man wearing saffron robes and a holy Rudraksha string on his hand, was going to pay his respects at Pedro Baba's Tomb.

A few recognised him as the well known Don Purshottam Panara. Word spread and the beggars around the tomb got to hear the news and all of them gathered around the tomb. The moment Vakil Saab ventured out, all of them gathered around him and Vakil Saab started distributing money to the poor. Just then Vakil Saab received a message on his mobile phone, saying that the drug dealer Shivram from Porbunder was killed in an encounter with the police. This news was a little strange, since Shivram had very good relations with Gujarat police. The police who survived on the cash doled out by Shivram, had killed him. It was really surprising. (At this juncture I, as a writer would like to add, that it is not good either to be a friend with the police nor is it to be a foe.)

Within twenty four hours Rampal proved that he had influential friends in all corners, if he needed them. Vakil Saab understood that Shivram was killed, because of Rampal's influence. Rampal too wanted to destroy anybody who believed in spilling blood. Rampal had made the smartest people scratch their heads with his clever moves and he was not ready to open up about how he had done this.

All of the mafia from Porbundar were still wondering how Gujarat police could kill Shivram, their own man.

Shevantilal went underground and Nandu Merai was in hiding. Both of them were as vile and slimy as a fox. Looking for them was like searching for a needle in a haystack. Bhau's gang was a mixture of people who did not have any morals or principles in life.

Aadil's relatives were pitched in at the hospital and he was going closer to death with every passing second.

A man capable of tearing a lion apart was lying in bed powerless and oblivious of what was happening around him. His Ammi and Abbu could not stop their tears. They were constantly praying for him. Nasreen could not bear to look at her dearest friend in this state and she too was praying and reading the holy book. Vakil Saab had once again started reciting the Mrutyunjay Jaap sitting in a room in the Hospital. He wanted to save Aadil at any cost.

Just then Rampal received important news; suspended Inspector Nandu Merai had driven the killers to Vakil Saab's office. Rampal lost his temper and his blood was boiling when he heard this and he was ready to kill them.

The Media waiting outside the hospital was keeping track of everything happening at the hospital. They could think a step ahead of everybody. They knew that if Aadil did not survive then nobody could stop the gang war in Mumbai. Meanwhile at the hospital they were desperately trying to bring Aadil's blood pressure down. All the Doctors and Nurses were running in a frenzy around Aadil's room and suddenly there was silence in the corridor. The doctors emerged from the room and gave a statement, "Aadil is no more." Vakil Saab sat still for a few moments but his eyes were filled with tears. A whirlwind of emotions was slowly raising its head in his heart and it was going to destroy his enemies completely. Vakil Saab did not believe in bloodshed, but just now he was ready to kill the person who was the reason for Aadil's death.

The newspaper's headlines the next day read "Purshottam Panara's Son Passes Away." The moment the news spread all over Mumbai, people were waiting in anticipation of what would come next. Mumbai was sitting on a heap of dynamite, ready to blast at any second. A live telecast had started from just outside the Hospital and the media was waiting to get inside Vakil Saab's room. They were waiting for the first bit of news and were eager to ask that one question. Aadil was your son and who do you hold responsible for his death? Vakil Saab was not ready to talk with anybody.

Aadil's relatives were grieving for Aadil's death at the hospital. Gurudas and Nasreen were bravely handling Aadil's Abbu and Ammi and they were crying uncontrollably. Aadil's body was given to the parents for religious formalities after four hours. The ambulance reached the house and they saw that the whole area was full of mourners, waiting to have a look at Aadil. Everyone, be it a Muslim or Hindu, was mourning for Aadil. All the shops in the area were shut down in respect. He was everyone's favourite. The media had a crew waiting here too. Vakil Saab was surrounded by his security. He did not want to answer any of their questions.

They bathed Aadil to prepare him for his final trip, to meet his god almighty, which is called 'Supurde Khak' in

Aadil's religion. Vakil Saab covered his body with flowers. Abbu and Ammi were being supervised by the Doctors as instructed by Vakil Saab, as their most beloved son was going to be buried. This was difficult to bear for anyone.

The first one to give their shoulder to the bier was Vakil Saab and Gurudas. The streets were teeming with mourners accompanying the funeral. The police had to lathi charge to keep the crowd in check. The funeral procession reached Mahim Cemetry with great difficulty and the relatives recited the Fatiha, a muslim prayer read before the burial. Aadil was laid to rest for his final journey.

Vakil Saab bent down and took the soil in his hand and swore that he will not rest till he makes his killers suffer. The storm raging in Vakil Saab's heart would die down only after he killed those murderers. He did not ask Rampal anything nor did he share his own feelings with him.

The main culprit behind this war was "Chilli Poison Drug" and the main person responsible for all this was Zakir, who was ruling the drug world in Dubai. Zakir was a promiscuous and lewd man selling cheap drugs in India, Pakistan, Bangladesh and Nepal. He was making the future generation hollow with his poison and in exchange he was living a life of luxury. He was sitting on a heap of illicit wealth gained by illegal means. Vakil Saab's main goal in life now was to shake up Zakir's foundation and put an end to his illegal activities. Vakil Saab could not wait to take his revenge but unnecessary hurry could spoil his game. Vakil Saab wanted to work with patience and care. He knew that neither force nor money was going to destroy Zakir. His weakness was the only thing which could destroy him and soon he knew his weakness was "women." He was a filthy lech, always thinking about sex and women.

Vakil Saab thought with his businessman brain and planned his strategy to trap Zakir. To start his battle he chose Raja Ajmeri and Qyum Ejaaz as his weapons to destroy him. They wore branded clothes and spoke sophisticated English like the Britishers. Many were fooled into giving up even the clothes on their back by their smooth talking. They had impeccable manners, nobody could find fault in their etiquette. Even the way they presented themselves was very polished and they were very handsome and regal in their appearance.

They demanded five crores for Zakir's life. Though it was a big sum Vakil Saab agreed to it without batting an eyelid. In his heart five crores was not a big sum to pay for his vendetta for Aadil's life. Raja Ajmeri and Qyum Ejaz were men of their word. They considered loyalty of the utmost importance in their heart, even more than wealth. At the same time their minds were sharp like a vile fox and they were experts at their job. They had planned to destroy Zakir without any bloodshed. They had checked his background and planned his journey into oblivion. He had all the characteristics of a debaucherous man and he loved Indian and Pakistani Girls as his companions. He did not enjoy foreigner's company.

Raja Ajmeri and Qyum Ejaz left for Dubai with weapons for Zakir's doom in tow. A South Indian girl, Madhubala, who worked in C Grade films, was accompanying them. She was chosen for her voluptuous figure and her thundering thighs which matched her heavy heaving bosom. Any man would turn to look at her twice. Her wheatish complexion, her pearl-like teeth gleaming through her smile and dimpled cheeks added to her beauty. She looked like an angel but she was a devil, brought here to entice Zakir. Though she was pretty she was sold for a few rupees into the trade, but today Raja Ajmeri and Qyum Ejaz had paid her well, as they needed her for their business.

The three of them got off at Dubai airport and arrived at the Hotel. Now the plan was put into action. Soon they received news that Zakir often goes to a club in Fujera near Dubai, in the evenings. He enjoyed smoking the Hookah there. All three of them made a plan and reached Fujera and booked a table in a club called Arabian nights. Zakir travelled all the way from Bur Dubai to Fujera just to smoke Hookah in peace and buy the beauties he liked. The clubs in Bur Dubai were always crowded, so he avoided them and went to Fujera.

Raja, Qyum and Madhubala were smoking hookahs at the club. They were waiting for Zakir's arrival. Zakir arrived after two hours in his BMW and the moment he arrived the men in the club started flaunting the girls. Raja Ajmeria and Qyum Ejaz were watching all this. The moment they saw a window of opportunity they grabbed it and sent Madhubala closer to Zakir. Zakir looked at Madhubala and Madhubala put her hand out and wished Zakir. She said "Good evening." The moment Zakir took her hand in his, he was smitten by her. Madhubala said with a sweet smile "I am a tourist here. I want to earn a little money. Please give me a chance to please you. You will never forget me." In an instant Zakir was lost in the whirlpool of her eyes. The moment he saw her brown skin and sexy body his eyes were brimming with lust. It seemed as if he would eat her alive with his eyes. Both of them were puffing away at the Hookah together and after some time both of them left the club together. Raja Ajmeri and Qyum Ejaz left the club after them and went to their hotel. Madhubala spent the night in Zakir's lustful arms. By the time she was back at the hotel, not only had she won Zakir's trust but had earned a couple of Dinars too. She had promised him she would return the next evening.

During the day Raja Ajmeri and Qyum Ejaz were trying to obtain Chilly Poison. The plan was that Madhubala would add a little bit of it to every peg she poured for him, which would eventually end his life.

They had to struggle a lot but finally they got the drug. Madhubala slept during the day and when she left in the evening to meet him again, she was fresh as a blossoming flower. She looked beautiful. Madhubala was given instructions on how she was supposed to mix Chilly Poison in his drink, when Zakir was busy with her. She reached Zakir's sex haven as per the plan. Madhubala's statement that "You will never forget me" was accurate. Zakir was longing to hold Madhubala in his arms again. He was dreaming about Madhubala's sexy figure all day. He was waiting impatiently to see her again and the moment she arrived he took her straight to the bedroom.

The moment they settled on the bed Madhubala started flattering him with her smooth talk and at the same time she was massaging his body too. The massage made the lecherous Zakir lose his senses. Madhubala filled two pegs of his drink for him. It was decided earlier that Chilly Poison will be mixed in the third peg without his knowledge. The fourth peg would have a little more of the drug and the fifth peg would be the last nail in Zakir's coffin. And that was exactly how it was happening. They had to finish Zakir today without fail and in the investigation it should be clear that he died from an overdose of Chilly Poison.

Everything was moving according to their plan. Zakir was drinking one peg after the other. Madhubala was flattering him in such a way with her massage and her touch, that his lust crossed all the limits. Just then she whispered in his ears "You can enjoy this only if you are a savage. Today, drink a lot and then make savage love to me. I am waiting for you." Zakir's lust knew no bounds after listening to Madhubala's sexy voice in his ears. She kept refilling his drink which was mixed with Chilly Poison now. He was losing his senses and was finding Madhubala more beautiful than ever. While Madhubala was adding more Chilly Poison to his drinks, he was telling her "I will make you my Queen." Madhubala looked at him mischievously and said "come let's take a shower together." She took him to the washroom and started to fill the bathtub with water. By this time Zakir had started to lose his mind. Madhubala helped him get into the tub. Within seconds he had lost his senses completely.

Once again Madhubala handed him a drink and said "drink my lord, drink for my sake." Zakir took a few sips and he started to drown in the bathtub. Madhubala was observing him struggling for breath and then she saw him going under the water and the bubbles coming up. The Drug Lord had died in a watery grave by the same drugs which he was selling to kill others. When Madhubala was sure that he had stopped breathing, she immediately left for the hotel and all three went to the airport to catch the next flight for Mumbai. Madhubala had earned a big amount from Zakir anyway and she also received very costly gifts from Raja Ajmeri and Qyum Ejaz. The mission was completed with such finesse that nobody could doubt them. Raja and Qyum thanked God that they got a chance to kill a drug lord.

The next day, the Gulf news carried the headline, "Zakir dies of an overdose." The crime world was shaken by this news. It was unbelievable that a horrible man like Zakir would end his existence by simply an overdose of the same drug he was selling. The Dubai police gave a statement that "Zakir died in the bathtub after consuming alcohol." The postmortem report also said that Zakir died due to alcohol and drugs.

Rampal was shocked. Vakil Saab had managed to kill a drug lord like Zakir from across the seven seas, without anybody's help. Zakir's death immediately after Aadil's death meant that the war had started. Bhau's heart was fluttering with fear at his Bungalow, though he had total security all around. All his dreams were completely shattered. Vakil Saab had opened the account from his side and had managed to finish his job silently and stealthily. The media spent the whole day guessing the reason behind Zakir's death.

The next day Rampal rushed to Vakil Saab's room. He wanted to inform Vakil Saab that Nandu Merai was murdered by someone. Vakil Saab was meditating, his eyes closed, facing God Shiva with the Japmala in his hand. He was wearing a saffron lungi and a string of the holy beads Rudraksha around his neck. He had washed his saffron kurta and put it to dry and it was still damp.

Rampal could not understand why he needed to wash his clothes at this hour of the night, since he never washed his clothes himself. Vakil Saab opened his eyes as he heard the sound of Rampal's feet. Rampal informed Vakil Saab urgently "Nandu Merai was murdered last night." Vakil Saab was silent after hearing the news and closed his eyes again. It was as if he knew about the murder or he himself had planned it.

The police also suspected the Vakil gang, as they were his only enemy, but they kept quiet as they did not have any proof. Vakil Saab was the Bhishma Pitamah of the legal world. He was a strict disciplinarian and even the police were silently supporting him in a way. Rampal stood there for sometime and left the room quietly. He was now sure that Nandu Merai was killed by Vakil Saab. The countdown of Aadil's killers had begun.

Four years ago, the drug dealers were so brave that they sold drugs just outside the police quarters to make their children addicts. A boy from Aadil's area lost his life because of his drug addiction. Losing a young son made his mother lose her mind. A drug called "Double V" was very popular in those days and it was in demand in Bandra West more than in Bandra East. "Double V" meant two brothers Vasim and Waris, the two brothers who dealt in drugs. Aadil could not bear that mother's pain. He immediately landed at Vasim and Waris' house. The brothers depended on the boys of the locality for their business. They thought nobody could touch them. Aadil managed to grab both the boys from their protection ring, tied them to his bike and dragged them on the road. When both of them were half dead he left them on the road. The police reached after Aadil's exit and admitted them to the hospital. When the police were inquiring about the assault they refused to divulge any names and Aadil's name was not mentioned as they were too scared of him. They pissed their pants whenever his name was mentioned.

As a result of this incident many panwallahs outside schools and colleges stopped selling drugs in their shops as they were terrified of Aadil. Aadil was a hero for millions of peace loving people, so when people heard about his death they were heart-broken.

Zakir's death had made the Indian and Pakistani drug dealers orphans. They may not have cried as much for their parents' death, as they were crying for Zakir. Trillions of cash turnover was turned into dust by Vakil Saab. A simple man who neither owned a big gang nor did he make a run to save himself from the police, had orphaned the drug dealers of Asia with a single snap of his fingers. Everybody was talking about Vakil Saab now. He was split into two halves in his own country. On one side the mafia were ready to kill him, on the other side the peace loving population were praying for his safety.

When Vakil Saab heard what Rampal said, he closed his eyes and continued to meditate. His face looked calm as if he was sitting in the lap of the Himalaya mountains. After the murder of two important people, it seemed as if the fire of vengeance in his heart had simmered down a little.

Rampal wanted to ask him so many questions. But when he looked at Vakil Saab's stern face, he could not muster the courage to do so and this was suffocating for him. He felt very lonely after Aadil's death. Vakil Saab was lost in his own world and Gurudas had almost broken his relationship with the world of crime. He was now busy with films and film production. The Vakil gang had invested crores in the film he was making with Nasreen. Gurudas wanted the film to do well and reach the hundred crore club at the box office. Nasreen too was conscious about the responsibility she was carrying and she was working hard for it.

Nasreen considered Gurudas as her companion, whom she loved immensely. And she was perfect for him too. God very rarely gifts one person with so many virtues. She was beautiful, very clear in her thoughts and very kind hearted too. She had almost broken down after Aadil's death. But she gathered herself and took care of Aadil's Ammi and Abbu. Nasreen had decided that it was her duty now to take care of Aadil's parents as long as they lived. Although she had a busy schedule, she spent a little time every morning and evening with them. She always regretted that Aadil would not be present to see the release of her first film. But that is Destiny. The show must go on. Both Nasreen and Gurudas believed in this philosophy. They were running the rat race of Bollywood with their eyes closed and they were determined to win this race. They had every right to join the Bollywood Caravan as they had earned their place in it.

On the other hand it was easy to guess that Vakil Saab's next victim would be either Shevantilal or Bhau and Bhau was well aware of this. He had become vigilant and alert too. He was in high spirits because he thought he had a huge army of criminals supporting him. Rampal Satardekar was finding it a little difficult to find Bhau's cronies. Bhau was in a hurry now to end this cat and mouse game. He was sure that he was going to win. He had shaken hands with all the drug mafias of the world. Because of this his status was rising in their eyes.

He now had a very high-end security agency protecting him and was surrounded by bodyguards, twenty four seven. He knew how Vakil Saab had a heart of a lion, who did not think of the consequences of his actions. So Bhau transformed his bungalow into an impenetrable castle, where even a bird could not fly in without his permission. After making the drug mafia his friends, he was climbing the rungs of success one by one. He had always lived a life of humiliation in the eyes of his wife and son. And now the word was that he was one of the most important people within the drug mafia. He considered himself an ace in the world of crime. He had convinced himself that he would win this fight. But in his heart of hearts he was still very scared of Vakil Saab.

Certain police personnel were helping Bhau but there were also police personnel who had a liking for Vakil Saab. They had informed him that a strong case was being built up against him with the help of the Crime Branch and the warrant was not bailable. It carried allegations that Purshottam Pansara aka Vakil Saab was a drug mafia of Mumbai, he was involved in the flesh trade of young girls and to add to that he was also dealing in illegal arms and ammunition. The warrant also claimed that Vakil Saab demanded extortion money from business owners. These allegations could send him to jail for life. When Rampal Satardekar heard about this, his blood started boiling. He could not believe that such allegations were being made against Vakil Saab. This turn of events was totally unexpected. There was surely somebody big supporting Bhau. Rampal wanted to warn Vakil Saab as soon as possible about what was happening against him so that he could take precautions. He rushed towards Vakil Saab's room. Rampal found him sleeping peacefully and a lamp was burning in front of Lord Shivji's temple, which meant that he had prayed to Shivji before laying down to sleep. The light from the lamp was flooding his room. The Rudraksha beads on his wrist, which were given to him by the Mahatma from Kailash, were sparkling like the Naagmani jewels. They had a different shine of their own. This visual was breathtaking. Rampal wanted to keep this miraculous vision close to his heart. He did not wish to share it with anybody. That Rudraksha string was worth more than the Kohinoor Diamond in this moment. Vakil Saab was evolving into a different personality after Aadil's death. He had an aura around him. His face looked peaceful. There was no anger, no lust, no jealousy and no hatred in his demeanour. He looked as if a deity had taken a human form. This difference in Vakil Saab's behaviour baffled Rampal Satardekar and his own life path seemed aimless.

At the moment it was difficult to trust any news. Rampal had also received news that the enemies were using Shevantilal as a scapegoat to kill Vakil Saab. Rampal was afraid that the way VakilSaab had killed Nandu Merai in the darkness of the night, the same way he may kill Shevantilal. This thought troubled Rampal and he decided to sit near Vakil Saab and keep an eye on him.

Rampal woke up with the sound of birds early in the morning. He looked around the room. Vakil Saab was still in deep sleep. Rampal kept a vigil outside Vakil Saab's room everyday without fail. This went on for fifteen days. The enemies were ready to pounce and were tired of waiting for Vakil Saab to go out alone in the night. During those fifteen days, Vakil Saab finished making his Will. Nobody knew what was given to whom. Both Rampal and Gurudas were worried and wondered why was it necessary for Vakil Saab to make a Will. They did not have the heart to ask Vakil Saab about it. They were making a futile attempt to read his expressions and they were unsuccessful at it. Every day Rampal and Gurudas saw a new facet of Vakil Saab's personality. They felt as if they were meeting a new man every day.

During this period Vakil Saab's cook, Kunj Bihari came to Vakil Saab's office. Rampal wondered about this and asked Kunj Bihari why had he come there. He said, "Vakil Saab's mother has not been eating well since a few days. I have to force her to eat and you know very well that I have the responsibility to look after the whole house. So one day I took Mataji to the family doctor. Everything was checked and the reports were normal. So one day I asked her "Mataji you are healthy, then why do you eat so little." So she said "Arre.. you are worrying unnecessarily Kunj. I eat less so that I can go to my God, my Kanha soon. So I asked her "But why Mataji? Are you tired of Vakil Saab and all of us too? So she said "Arre are you mad. Now my body is old. How long will you water a dried tree Kunj? Now I slowly want to leave this body."

The Jain community has a ritual called Santhara where they voluntarily, slowly reduce their intake, withdraw all physical and mental activities and leave their body peacefully to meet their Lord. Santhara means that you are reducing the possibility of rebirth while doing good Karma too.

Similarly Mataji passed many days, surviving only on water, to attain salvation. She constantly talked about meeting her Lord Krishna.

Hearing this news worried Rampal and he immediately narrated this to Vakil Saab. Vakil Saab left his office and went to meet his Mother at once. Rampal and Kunj Bihari were also accompanying him. When they reached home, Mataji was sitting in her bed counting the strings of beads in her hand, with Lord Krishna on her mind. Mataji had lost a lot of weight yet her face had an ethereal quality. It was shining. The moment they entered, both of them touched her feet as usual with respect. Mataji looked at Kunj Bihari and said "So you complained about me to Purshottam?"

"No Maa, Kunj Bihari has not complained. I just felt like seeing you. Maa, why have you stopped eating."

Maataji lovingly put her hand on Vakil Saab's head and softly said, "Son, my body is getting old now."

Shariram yad avapnoti yach chapy utkramatishvarah

Grihitvaitani sanyati vayur gandhan ivashayat

It is written in Gita that "the soul is immortal so the soul needs a new body. The way the wind carries the smell of a perfume the same way God transfers the soul into another body with all the senses taken with it. So now this soul needs to fly away and transfer to another body."

After hearing this Vakil Saab said "But Maa all of us will be orphans."

Mataji replied "Everybody has to go when the time comes." She looked at the picture hanging on the wall in which Lord Krishna was reciting a sermon to Arjun. When she saw it she told Vakil Saab "Purshottam I know there is a war of emotions raging in your heart and you still have to fight all your battles. Many depend on you for their existence. You don't worry about me and get ready for your battle. You will definitely win."

Mataji repeated what Lord Krishna had told Arjun before the Mahabharata War started. She said "Pick up your Gandiv(Arjun's bow) and initiate the war. You have the Great Yogeshwar with you."

When Rampal Sataedekar heard all this, he could almost hear the sound of the Conch, preparing them for the war ahead. He thought to himself "Mothers who give birth to such great sons are blessed." After hearing what his Mataji was telling him he realised that what his mother says is correct. This world is but an illusion.

A month had passed since. Today Vakil Saab was a little uneasy and worried. This uneasiness motivated him to go and meet his mother. Rampal as usual was sleeping in the room outside. The moment he heard the shuffle of Vakil Saab's feet, he got up with the revolver in his hand and started following Vakil Saab. Quietly tiptoeing behind him. Vakil Saab's Rolls Royce stopped in front of Mataji's house. When Vakil Saab reached inside, he saw Mataji sleeping on a mat on the floor. There was a single lamp burning beside her yet the whole room was filled with light. The light was emitting out of Mataji's face, as she had reached a higher level of spirituality. Kunj Bihari was reciting the fifteenth Adhyay of Geeta for Mataji. Vakil Saab instantly understood that it was time to bid farewell to his beloved mother. He sat down and put her head in his lap. The moment the fifteenth Adhayay finished, Maa's soul left for the heavenly abode. Kunj Bihari was crying bitterly and was telling Vakil Saab "Vakil Saab maa has left us all. We are orphans now."

Vakil Saab sat still, with her head in his lap, looking peaceful.

Eleven Brahmins were called for the cremation. While the Brahmins recited the Holy Mantras she was laid to rest with forty kilos of Sandalwood burning her mortal body into ashes. It was a regal farewell befitting a mother of a king like Purshottam Pansara.

Rampal did not need to safeguard Vakil Saab anymore. He knew that Vakil Saab would not step out alone at night now.

The Amavasya (new moon night) arrived. It was considered an omen of bad luck. Vakil Saab saw that Rampal was in deep sleep on his bed. He left the house in darkness with a revolver in his hand. The morning brought the sad news. The Mumbai police Commissioner was murdered. Rampal ran to see where Vakil Saab was, but he was not to be found.

The police were quickly trying to blockade all the roads, so that they could arrest Vakil Saab. They were sure that Vakil Saab had murdered the police Commissioner. CCTV footage also showed Vakil Saab standing outside the Commissioner's house, with a revolver in his hand. When Vakil Saab came out of the Commissioner's house, he was seen holding a few files and a revolver in his hand and the Commissioner's body could be seen lying in the background.

That meant that there was no footage to show him murdering the Commissioner. As he had not installed CCTV inside the house. The police surrounded Vakil Saab's house and started the search operation. They searched every room in the house but they could not find Vakil Saab. They even sealed a few rooms. This was no small matter, as the Commissioner of Mumbai police was murdered.

Vakil Saab had left his Mobile at home so that the police could not track his location; as he had a lot of pending work to finish. The police was equally dumbfounded and confused about the murder as Rampal and Gurudas. They did not expect Vakil Saab to do something so drastic. But they did now know that Vakil Saab had started the last battle of his life.

The previous Dons of Mumbai would always strike their enemies with the help of their colleagues. Making a big name while hiding behind their backs. But Vakil Saab did not want any of his colleagues to commit a crime for his sake. He was fighting on the battlefield single handedly. In other words he could be called Rambo.

After the Commissioner's murder they could not trace Vakil Saab. They raided Reshma Billi's house too but she did not have an inkling of the whole episode. The police were totally confused and could not solve the how, the what and the where of this murder mystery. This was taking longer and they felt that it was a waste of their time.

Then suddenly Gurudas, Rampal and Reshma were called to the police Station and grilled for hours. This too turned out to be a waste of time. Then an idea hit them and they started questioning the Commissioner's Family. None of the family members were present in the house when the Commissioner was murdered. They were staying at his Farm house as the Commissioner preferred to stay alone. His wife and son did not know anything about the files Vakil Saab had taken with him. But the wife and son's lavish lifestyle proved that just the Commissioner's pay was not enough for all this. The farmhouse had all the signs of an opulent and fancy lifestyle. A large swimming pool, imported cars and an army of servants to boot.

Certain files were found in the Commissioner's house in the name of a high profile lady, Ayesha, who was popular in the party circuit. After a detailed investigation they found that she was his business partner and she had invested a big amount in some projects. He had mostly invested in land and the police did not find much cash in his house, except for three lakhs. This was not a very big amount but a diary was found along with the cash, with a few names written in it and every name had a dollar sign before the name. This diary carried the information which was the main reason of murder.

The Commissioner had given the liberty of selling drugs to his cronies through this dollar sign. But he had not realised that many children of the police family were also addicted to these drugs.

The police started interrogating Ayesha and she answered these questions in her own style and panache. She said that she was doing business with different people and had invested money too. Her C.A. who was accompanying her, gave all the investment copies to the police to scan. The police had deciphered the fact that Ayesha was an expert at dubious practices. She had her fingers in all the pies of the immoral world, so she treaded very carefully. She showed that all her deals were clear cut and spotless. When the police asked her how much she knew about the murder she replied "I know as much as anybody knows." They asked her when did she last meet the Commissioner. She was silent for a while and then she remembered the cameras in the lobby. The memory made her blurt out the truth.

The police asked her again "Why did you meet the Commissioner three days prior to his murder." Ayesha replied that it was a routine meeting and they often met for business. The police understood the reason why the Commissioner did not have cameras in that room. It was to cover up their scandalous meetings.

The police were scanning the investment copies thoroughly and they managed to find a strange condition written in it. The condition was that if a partner dies during the period of partnership then the living partner will become the sole owner of the property. The police found this condition very weird. When the police asked her about it, she replied very calmly "This agreement has been signed by both me and the Commissioner and this condition was added by the Commissioner himself." The police could not deny the fact that the agreement had both their signatures. This brought Ayesha under the radar of the police investigation.

All the places which were under police suspicion were raided but they all proved futile. Bhau was terrified after the Commissioner's murder. He stopped Rupesh Kumar from venturing out completely. Bhau was very sure that either him or Shevantilal were Vakil Saab's next targets. Shevantilal too was changing his residence every day, as he was fearing for his life too. He was not only a target of Vakil Saab but the police too. He was so tense, he had not slept peacefully for many days and his willpower was slowly breaking down. At times he thought of surrendering to the police to put an end to his misery and then he pacified himself by thinking "Anyway this Vakil is going to die soon."Bhau had deployed hit men to kill Vakil Saab and the police were after his life too. The moment Vakil dies everything would settle according to Bhau's plan. Then the police and the goons would be hand in glove and they could commit crimes together and rule over the whole of Mumbai." Shevantilal passed his time with these empty and useless thoughts.

Vakil Saab's sole aim in life was to finish off Bhau and Rupesh kumar, as he wanted to avenge Aadil's murder and he could rid Mumbai of the drugs mafia. Vakil Saab was in no hurry to kill Shevantilal, as his way of operating his business was different and he played with the pawns in his game the crooked way. He would first kill the King in his game and then the Bishop. The same way he killed Zakir first and then the Commissioner and in the end the knight and the pawns would die in the battle which ensued.

Ayesha realised soon that she could not save herself from the hands of the police for too long. She was very impressed by Vakil Saab's personality and was secretly in love with him. But she knew that he only belonged to Reshma. Ayesha put all the cards on the table and confessed everything to Vakil Saab unconditionally.

The Mumbai drugs mafia worked thanks to the Commissioners mercy and Ayesha was the only one who knew about this secret information. The Commissioner had blurted all his secrets to her when he had downed a few pegs and was lost in her beauty. He found peace in Ayesha's arms and they spent many nights together. This was also one of the many reasons to not put up a camera inside the house.

Ayesha was very pretty at the age of thirty six. She had everything needed for a lavish life, yet she felt lonely at times. When she looked out of her high rise balcony she saw the blue Arabian Sea on one side and when she turned her head to look on the other side, she saw an ocean of people swirling around. She felt that she was lonely in this melee, even though she was surrounded by hordes of people. There was nobody she could call her own. She longed to have a child sired by Vakil Saab, so that she would have somebody to look after her in her old age. This was her inner feeling but she could not escape the facts of her life. When she felt lonely she would drink, so that she would not feel isolated and she could drown herself in her intoxication.

Ayesha poured herself drink and took a sip and as the alcohol slowly slid down her beautiful neck, she felt at peace. She picked up the file lying on the table and started turning the pages. Now she was the sole owner of the land and it was worth crores of rupees. She smiled a little but her smile was full of vanity as she looked at her growing list of possessions. She always thanked her beauty for whatever she had achieved. Her celestial beauty turned the biggest braggers into innocent blabbering boys. The men found heaven when she enveloped them in her arms, resting their heads on her bosom and she made them pay a huge amount for that.

As she was stroking the glass in her hand, her mind went back into her past, down the memory lane. She went back to the time when she stayed in a small town. There was a liquor dealer in that village with whom she spent a night and she chose to increase her own value. Hearing her price the dealer abused her and told her "I will decide your price. You are just a two bit whore." This shocked Ayesha and she lost her sleep over it for many days. Since then she never allowed any man to decide her worth. She wanted to forget those unpleasant times. She gulped down her drink in a split second to drown her past.

Vakil Saab knew Ayesha well. He was well aware that she was a sad soul and he also knew that she wanted to build a mountain of wealth so huge that nobody dared to evaluate her existence. Vakil Saab took advantage of her feelings and assessed the Commissioners daily routine with her help. She simply followed Vakil Saab's instructions and in return she made a huge amount of wealth in her own name, just like she wanted to. Wealth has a funda (fundamental principal) of its own. People sell their peace of mind to make more money and barely use thirty percent of it for their own needs. The remaining seventy percent is usually usurped by their own people through flattery or it lies unused in some basement, as it cannot be disclosed. Ayesha ignored all these thoughts. She did not want her hunger for wealth to die down. She wanted to reach the top most peak of fame.

Vakil Saab was still out of police reach. Rampal and Gurudas did not know his whereabouts either. Though the police were a little disappointed, they were sure about one thing; Bhau's son Rupesh Kumar was Vakil Saab's next target. Vakil Saab was keen on avenging his son Aadil's murder at any cost, and to do that he would have to come to Bhau's residence. The police were on high alert and they were sure that Bhau would be murdered in the night.

Bhau had set up strong security from his side. Suddenly one day a package arrived with a note saying that payment was already made for it. When Bhau opened the package, it contained all the items needed for a funeral. Bhau was livid and he started hitting the man who had come to deliver. Just then Bhau's phone started ringing. Bhau answered the phone and before he could utter a word in his tense state of mind, Vakil Saab spoke "Bhau did you receive the things needed for the funeral?" On hearing Vakil Saab's voice Bhau started shaking. He looked around his room with fear and saw the police guarding him. He realised that he was in his own house and did not need to fear anybody. Vakil Saab was a murderer and the police were after his life. Bhau gathered courage and said "Vakil you have made things easy for me. You did me a favour by killing the Commissioner. Now you will either hang by the neck or will be killed by police bullets. You sent the funeral items at the wrong address. It should have reached your house instead of mine. You are close to your death Vakil." Vakil replied "No doubt about it. I'm ready for my death with a shroud tied to my head anyway. But I will be at peace when your son's funeral procession leaves your house tomorrow. That will be a true homage to my son's death." Within a span of a few minutes, the police managed to trace Vakil Saab's call location and the streets of Mumbai were echoing with the sound of sirens. Vakil Saab knew exactly what to do and he was moving as fast as the hands of a clock. Vakil Saab took off from his location before the police could reach him. The police searched the location for hours, checking every building, but it turned out to be futile. Vakil Saab was showing the police that he was one up in their game.

Bhau ramped up the security in his bungalow. No stranger was allowed in the house now. Rupesh Kumar also stayed in his room. Both Rupesh and Bhau were very scared of Vakil Saab's threat. Bhau could not sleep that night and he kept checking on Rupesh as he was worried about his safety.

The servant served Rupesh Kumar his breakfast with milk in his room at 10 am. At 11 am Bhau received a call on his mobile. It was Vakil Saab calling from a different number and a different location this time. The police were alert again and started tracing his location. But whatever Vakil Saab needed to say was very short. It did not give the police enough time to trace his call. Bhau was eager to hear what Vakil Saab wanted to say. Vakil Saab stated very calmly "Bhau, your son Rupesh Kumar is no more." The moment Bhau heard this he screamed, "Vakil have you lost your mind! The fear of police and being continuously on the run have driven you mad. Surrender to the police so that you can live in peace in jail for the rest of your life. If you don't, you will die a disgraceful death at the hands of the cops. Vakil Saab answered calmly, he said "Bhau you have always lived an over confident life. Sometimes I pity you. Just go and look. My vengeance is complete."

Bhau dropped the phone immediately and ran towards Rupesh's room. Rupesh was already dead. His whole body had turned blue and a bottle of Chilly Poison was lying near him. Rupesh had died because of an overdose of Chilly Poison. But this was shocking, as Rupesh never consumed drugs. He only had alcohol, so how did these drugs get here? Bhau was hysterical. Everybody in the house panicked. An ambulance was called and he was taken to J J hospital. The moment the Doctors looked at him they announced him dead on arrival.

The police started searching Bhau's house to find the loophole through which the drug had entered his house. As this incident happened within just one hour. The breakfast plate and his glass of milk were sent to the Forensic lab for testing.

Their cook Shiva Thapa, who always gave Rupesh Kumar his meals, was not to be found after Rupeshs' death. This made it clear that Shiva Thapa was the one who had mixed the Chilly Poison in his meal. Vakil Saab's mission was successful at every juncture. He had one more death written on his list.

The police were anyway troubled by Vakil Saab and now they had this Shiva Thapa to worry about. The identity proof for Shiva, given by Bhau's manager, all turned out to be fake. Even his name Shiva Thapa was not real. His photograph was sent to all the nearby railway stations and the airport, but Shiva Thapa had changed his appearance and left the country according to Vakil Saab's instructions.

His objective was to get to his village Chamba in Nepal. Once he had reached Chamba safely he would never have to work a day in his life. Vakil Saab had paid him generously. It was enough to take care of him and his future generations too.

Mumbai police was as efficient as the Scotland Yard. But today the foundation of Mumbai police had started to shake and Vakil Saab was instrumental in shredding their reputation to pieces. The police were trying their best to save their face. Gurudas, Rampal, Reshma and Nasreen's mobiles were tapped to trace Vakil Saab's whereabouts but Vakil Saab was overturning both the police and his enemies' plans. Earlier the police was under pressure from the State Government and now the Central Government had started pressuring them too. For the first time, the police informants were being royally pampered. They were fed a feast of Tandoori, Biryani and Chicken.

The headlines next morning read "End of a gang War. The Supposed Drug Dealer Killed." This headline had doubled the sales of the publication. The second line in the news read "Drug dealer commits suicide by hanging himself last night."

Bhau was frustrated after his son's death. He was drinking continuously. The police found him hanging by his neck above a king size bed covered with currency notes. Bhau had chosen this path of destruction himself. The Chilly Poison he was selling to others had destroyed his own family and killed his son in the bargain. The wealth he had amassed was of no use to anyone. Even though Bhau was known as one of the biggest drug dealers of Mumbai, the royal lifestyle, the luxury, everything burst like a bubble and there was nothing left now.

All of the small-time drug dealers were shocked by Bhau's death. A battle had come to an end. Bhau had always seen to his own benefit. He used people as pawns while playing his game and crushed them under his feet when he didn't need them anymore. His inherent nature was backstabbing people who were close to him. Now maybe Mumbai could be drug free. The whole chain of drug peddlers was almost broken after Bhau's death. First it was Zakir from Dubai, then the Commissioner and now Bhau.

The police were now expecting Vakil Saab to surrender after Bhau's death. Rampal and Gurudas were anticipating this too. So they gathered a big army of lawyers to fight Vakil Saab's battle, so that they could ask for an anticipatory bail. The police did not have any solid evidence for the Commissioner's murder. All they had was footage of Vakil Saab coming out of the commissioner's house with a revolver and some files. His fingerprints were not found anywhere in the forensic report. But a murder was committed and there definitely was a murderer hiding somewhere, yet to be found.

The police did not have any valid proof and they were trying to convince the media that Vakil Saab was the culprit, only on the basis of the CCTV footage. When the media questioned the police about how this was enough evidence to incriminate him, they were told that the police wanted to keep a few things private. The reality was that Vakil Saab had beat the police at every step.

A few more days passed but nobody could trace Vakil Saab and he did not contact any of his near and dear ones either.

Shevantilal had lost his mental balance. He looked dishevelled as he had not shaved or had a bath in many days. He was running from pillar to post in order to hide himself as he was scared of Vakil Saab and the police too. He had lost his mind and was running on the streets in a crazy state. Anybody who saw him would say "As you sow, so shall you reap."

Rampal and Gurudas were pressurising the informants to get Vakil Saab's whereabouts but all their attempts were fruitless. The days turned into weeks and weeks turned into months.

A year passed and the police heard that a group of Sadhus had come from U.P. and were residing in Bhandup, a Central Mumbai suburb. Somebody spread a rumour that Vakil Saab was hiding in that group. Without wasting time the police raided their Ashram. They arrested a man who had the same appearance and height as Vakil Saab and dragged him to the police station. They forcibly shaved off his beard and moustache. He protested loudly but the police did not hear his pleas. After all that they realised that they had made a mistake and the police force became a laughing stock. The angry Sadhu shaved his head off too and started a dharana in the police station. He threatened them with self immolation.

The other Sadhus also gathered outside the police station and shouted slogans against the police. The media too criticised the police. The Hindu organisation burnt down the police effigies. The newspapers were filled with police and Sadhu cartoons. After this ridicule the police were treading cautiously.

After Bhau's death, Vakil Saab too did not do anything drastic. It felt as if the war had come to an end. Rampal and Reshma searched all the sadhu's ashrams and akhadas all over India for a year. They could not find him anywhere. Wherever they went, they faced disappointment. Messages were sent to Vakil Saab through Electronic Media, "Please come back. All of us feel orphaned."

Vakil Saab's memories troubled Reshma the most. She had earned a name and wealth too, but the man whom she considered her true companion was not next to her. Vakil Saab was made of a different mettle and Reshma knew that he was a real hero. He took all problems in his stride and protected his friends.

With eyes downcast and bated breath, Reshma was still waiting for Vakil Saab. She would hum their songs in solitude. The same song which she used to sing for Vakil Saab, "Kuch toh log kahenge. Logo ka kaam hai kehna"

There were various rumours going around. Some said that Vakil Saab had committed suicide and some said he had millions of dollars in the Swiss banks, and he had escaped to an international destination. Some believed that he was living amongst them by changing his identity, so that he could come and meet Reshma in the middle of the night. The police also believed in that rumour and they posted their informant spies in the guise of drunkards, beggars and vagabonds around Reshma's house. The informants worked very hard for a few months but now the police believed in the fact that Reshma really knew nothing about Vakil Saab's whereabouts. All news was old news now.

The time had come close for Nasreen's film release. It was a Thursday, so she went to Pedro Baba's Dargah early in the morning to pay her respects. Today was a very important day in her life. Gurudas reached Vakil Saab's office after bowing down to Siddhi Vinayak Ganapati to pray for the film's success. There was a big crowd at the office. Reshma, Rampal and Aadil's Ammi and Abbu had come too, with hearts full of good wishes. Everybody wished that Nasreen's first film should be a big hit.

Media had surrounded Nasreen but she was answering all their questions confidently. In the midst of all this frenzy, Reshma was missing her dear friend Aadil very much. She could not change the fact that Aadil was no more. But Vakil Saab? He was still around… Why was he not sending any messages? What was the reason? Why was he so helpless? This mystery could be solved only after Vakil Saab's return. But again the same question… when will he be back?

Nasreen went to her neighbourhood and bowed down to all the elders, asking for their blessings. Today her first film was being released. A girl living in the chawls of Jogeshwari was going to shine on the silver screen as the lead actress. The most strange thing about it was that the publicity for the film had started in Jogeshwari chawl, not some famous studio.

Nasreen went to her grocery shop owner Shantilal Dungarshi, gave him a ticket and said "Shanti Uncle, please come, please see the film. Immediately he took out a toffee from his bottle and gave it to Nasreen and said "I will surely come my child. Celebrate your film with these sweets. After the release you will go and stay in Juhu." Nasreen replied "Shanti Uncle there is a very small distance between Jogeshwari and Juhu. You can come to visit me sometime Uncle. I too will come to meet you sometime." The milkman Dubey who had his shop next door said "Nasreen my child, you just watch… your name will reach sky high one day." Nasreen touched his feet and took his blessings.

Just then they could hear the sound of the Azan (a muslim prayer) in the background. Ramdhari said "See my child, even God agrees with us. This is his way of giving his blessings." Nasreen was a religious person at heart and the moment she heard the prayer, she covered her head with the Pallu (loose end of her sari) of her sari.

Gurudas looked at his watch. It was time for them to leave for the premier. Everybody left together for the PVR theatre. The media was waiting for the film's heroine. Gurudas had promoted this movie on a big scale. Big hoardings were put up on every nook and corner of Mumbai, with Nasreen's face shining in all her glory. Nasreen had travelled around the whole of India for the promotion of this film and had been to many reality shows too for promotion. Today the PVR theatre was going to witness a bevy of film stars from all over Mumbai for the premier. There was a big hullabaloo when Nasreen's lavish car arrived at the theatre. The moment she stepped out of the car she was bombarded with questions from every side.

"What is your character in this movie?"

"How do you feel about your very first movie?"

"Have you signed more films?" etc. etc.

Nasreen answered every question with great respect and with a beautiful smile on her face. The media was clicking pictures from all angles. As soon as the media interaction was over she was surrounded by fans and all of them wanted selfies with her. Slowly the crowd was getting uncontrollable and bouncers were called to escort Nasreen inside the theatre.

The film was a big hit from the very first show. Everybody's good wishes and Nasreen's sincerity had paid off. The film did a business of one crore in one week. A new era had begun. The stories of Gurudas and Nasreen started doing the rounds in the filmy world. Nasreen's popularity was reaching new heights and her price also went up with it. All the films produced by Gurudas had Nasreen as the Heroine. Both of them were climbing up the ladder of popularity together as their stars were shining brightly.

While all this was going on in Mumbai, a Swami Sadchitanand Saraswati Maharaj was giving a discourse in Prayagraj. Only the most pious souls get a chance to come to Kailash Mansarovar. It is believed that human existence was created in the Himalayas. The learned and the saints consider the Himalayas as Lord Shiva and the Mansarovar Lake as Mata Parvati. This lake was made by Lord Brahma himself, who is the creator of the world too. Thousands of saints, sages and learned ones were listening to Swami Sadchitanand's discourse. And among these pious sages sat Vakil Saab, listening peacefully with his eyes closed.

Since the last two years Vakil Saab was living a life of oblivion. His hair had grown thick and long. He was living anonymously, hiding behind his long beard and moustache. He was also wearing many strings of Rudraksha beads around his neck. Today he was a complete sage. The battle started by Vakil Saab had ended now. His whole life he had heard the echo of bullets in his ears. But now he felt immense peace. The sun had set on the demonic realm and it had come to an end now. Today was Shivratri, which is considered very pious according to all Hindus. On this pious day Vakil Saab took a bath in the icy cold river of Prayagraj and he left for Kailash. Now he had only one aim in his life and that was to be one with his creator. With every step he took towards it, he was singing 'Rudrashtakam' in his heart.

Namamisha Mishana Nirvana rupam

Vibhum vyapakam Brahma Veda-swaroopam

Nijam Nirgunam Nirvikalpam Nireeham

Chidakara makasa vasam Bhajeham

Lord Shiva is the epitome of all pious things and I bow down to you my Lord Shiva. He is present in all the particles of this Universe. I bow down to you again and again.

This was a prayer all Shiva devotees recite. With this prayer in his heart, he was moving ahead in life and had reached a high level of spirituality. His previous life was left far behind. He had already made his final will and had bequeathed his wealth to Gurudas, Rampal, Reshma and Nasreen equally. Now he had no attachments and no love for anything or anybody. He had transformed into a sage, on his path to penance. His every step took him closer to Kailash. He had left behind all the destructive storms and ear deafening shrieks of criminals. Trudging his tired body he was slowly getting closer to his creator. While walking on this lonely road covered with snow, Vakil Saab saw a little hut, partially covered in snowfall. It was a light snowfall, so Vakil Saab went towards the hut. A sadhu came out of the hut when he heard Vakil Saab's footsteps. When the sadhu looked at Vakil Saab, he saw an incredible shine on his face. The aura around him pleased the sadhu. Indians believe that guests who visit our house are a form of God and one should always welcome them. So the sadhu welcomed him inside his hut. Vakil Saab slowly entered the hut and the sadhu could see that his feet were swollen and his body was tired. He immediately made a Kadha (a herbal drink) and offered it to him. While he was drinking the Kadha the sadhu asked him about who he was. While talking to him the sadhu realised that this man looked very exhausted and asked him whether he could help him in anyway. He said "Dear sir, your feet are swollen and you look tired. Please let me massage your feet." Though Vakil Saab refused he still insisted and put his feet in his lap. Vakil Saab noticed that the sadhu had an immense desire to take care of him. While massaging his feet, the sadhu looked at Vakil Saab and asked "Maharaj, please tell me something about your life. I am very curious to know." Vakil Saab wondered what he should say to him, as he was on a path where there was no place for lies. So he simply said "I am just a common man. My life's aim is over so I am moving forward to meet my creator, the great Shiv."

The sadhu said "Maharaj i have something weighing down in my heart. Can I tell you my innermost thoughts." Vakil Saab said "I am obliged by your love and care. Please, you can tell me anything." The sadhu spoke slowly "I am a murderer. I killed my wife's lover. Later I realised that both of them really loved each other. I should have let them live their life happily and I should have moved on. She was not happy with me. Though she was with me in a physical state, she was not with me on a mental level. I felt very lonely. I suddenly felt as if I did not want any ties with this world. Now I feel at peace in this place, far away from the world. Still when I remember my actions, I get very disturbed and get distracted from my path towards God."

Vakil Saab saw that the burden of his guilt was weighing heavy on his heart. He said to him "Guilt can find its way to you even in a vast barren land if we have done something for selfish reasons and it follows us forever. Penance for our actions is the only way we can find peace within ourselves. Whether we committed those actions for selfish or unselfish reasons."

The sadhu felt a little relief when he heard Vakil Saab's advice. He decided to walk on the path of penance for the remaining journey of his life.

Then suddenly the sadhu asked him a question "Maharaj, have you ever committed a crime?"

Vakil Saab sat quietly for a few seconds and then answered "My whole life has been connected with crime. And if we are talking about murders, I have murdered many. But none of the murders were for selfish reasons. When there was a reign of terror, when the lower middle class was tortured and people suffered fraud, I punished those greedy, avaricious people who stole people's wealth. I have killed the drug mafia who sold drugs to kill the younger generation. I have been attracted to crime since childhood. I do not regret the murders I have committed. On the contrary I am happy. I have diligently and sincerely fought my share of battles that society sent my way"

As he was saying this Vakil Saab slowly got up and said "Now I must leave." The sadhu said "Maharaj, please stay for some time. It is still snowing." Vakil Saab looked outside the hut and said with a smile "I have to keep walking on the path that I have chosen" and he continued his journey on the cold road ahead. Leaving his footprints in the snow as he walked towards Kailash.

Without batting an eyelid, the sadhu continued looking at Vakil Saab walking away and in a span of a few seconds he had disappeared. Melted like the snow below his feet. His footprints had melted too. The sadhu felt like he had witnessed the union of the creation and the creator in front of his eyes. As if Vakil Saab's identity had merged with the snow laden mountains.

2040 – The New Beginning

The year is 2040. It is a new era, a new morning, a new world with new people, a new thought process and a new enthusiasm. Mumbai's skyline is filled with skyscrapers reaching for the clouds. Some of them are almost a hundred stories high. Many international companies have their offices here and they have made their colonies too. As the Metro network is spreading in all corners of Mumbai, travelling has become faster. It is easy to reach from one corner to the other within a few minutes. People are happy. Mumbai looks as clean and beautiful as Paris, thanks to the 'Cleanliness Drive' started a decade ago by a politician. All of the Mumbai Residents (Mumbaiites) are very loyal towards Mumbai.

Now almost fifty, the beautiful and graceful Nasreen, has made a big name in the film industry and has retired now, as she has other responsibilities. The partnership which began with a film with Gurudas has turned into a life partnership. Their love story has been cited as a sign of unity in India. They have a chubby little boy as a symbol of their love. He is named Purshottam in the memory of Vakil Saab. He is twelve now. The little lad often hears stories about Vakil Saab from his mother Nasreen. He often tells his Mother "I will be like Vakil Saab when I grow up and follow his footsteps" Vakil Saab was a leader, he fought the injustice done to people and lit a lamp in their dark life.

After a gap of twenty years Gurudas and Rampal are leading their separate lives. Gurudas received a big chunk of property as per Vakil Saab's will and now he is a well known producer in the film industry. Nasreen too played a big inning in the acting field and has a special room in her beautifully lavish bungalow, full of glittering awards she has won. Aadil's Abbu and Ammi are no more, but Nasreen looked after them till they lived.

Gurudas and Nasreen have started a charitable trust in Vakil Saab's name, to help society. People are still hoping that Vakil Saab will return one day. Since many years the poor are given food in Vakil Saab's memory on Shivratri Day, as he believed in Lord Shiva

Vakil Saab had ingested poison for the safety of the Vakil gang Just like Lord Shiva did and had distributed the drink of immortality (amrit) between Gurudas and Rampal. All the legal cases were still going on in Vakil Saab's absence and Gurudas had cleverly got him acquitted from them and now he was absolved of them all. He had regained his respect and his freedom too. Now he was independent and completely free.

Reshma Billi was now known as Reshma Aapa in the Music Industry. She spent her whole life waiting for Vakil Saab and now she only dressed in Pristine White in

Vakil Saab's memory. She also wore a string of Rudraksha beads in her neck and a big red bindi on her forehead. She looked like she was at peace and she had reached a different level of spirituality in her life. Her name had become synonymous with this image. Hard work and hours of music practice resulted in her popularity even in her growing years. She still sang melodiously and her voice was pleasing to the ear.

According to the Vakil Saab's will, a part of the property was given to Reshma, but she did not care for wealth, she loved Vakil Saab. She had visited all the temples, churches, masjids and also the gurudwaras, begging for his return. She often hums a song "People find God when they search for him with love. I just want my Beloved"

Mumbai has changed a lot but Vakil Saab's office has not changed much in all these years. It is eleven in the morning. A Rolls Royce arrives and stops in front of the office. The doorman opens the car door. An elderly man steps out of the car. He looks like he could be around sixty and he has a wiry body. He has a snow white beard and is wearing saffron robes. He walks straight to Vakil Saab's office. The moment he enters, he bows in front of Vakil Saab's photo frame and sits in the chair next to Vakil Saab's chair. Some poor people are standing outside the office in a line waiting for some charity. The man sitting on the chair says "Please send everybody in." He takes off his black sunglasses and puts them down on the table.

This is Vakil Saab's retainer Rampal. After Vakil Saab's exit, Rampal has been looking after Vakil Saab's throne. Just as Lakshman took care of Lord Rama's throne when Rama was in exile for fourteen years. He is still hoping for Vakil Saab's return and he is sure he will be back on his throne one day.

***

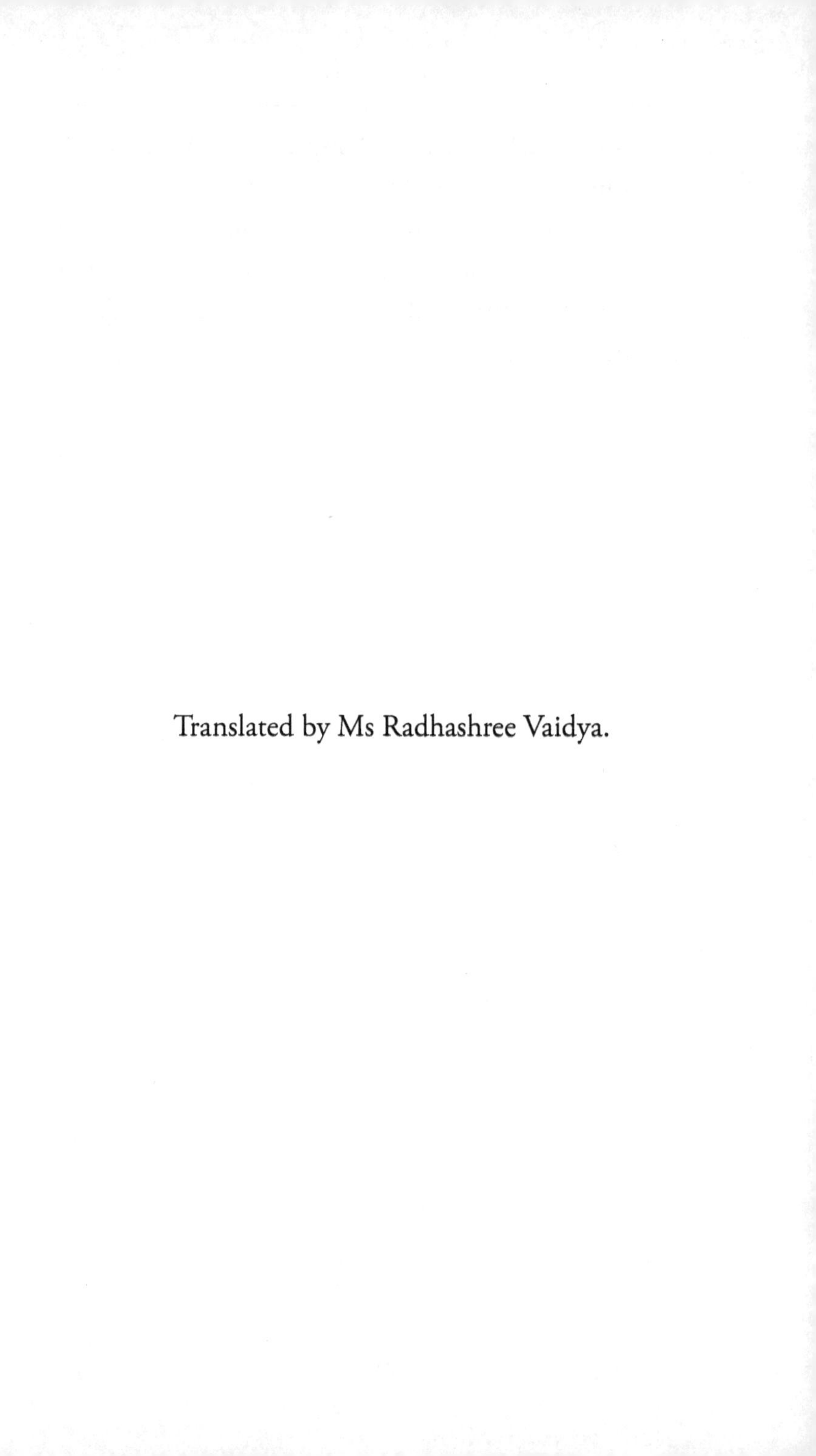

Translated by Ms Radhashree Vaidya.

If you have feedbacks about the book please drop an
email to **dineshlimbachiya1327@gmail.com**